From bump to baby and beyond...

Whether she's expecting or they're adopting,
a special arrival is on its way!

Follow the tears and triumphs as these couples find
their lives blessed with the magic of parenthood...

Look out for more BABY ON BOARD stories
coming soon from Harlequin Romance®!

Next month there is a
Boardroom Baby Surprise
from
Jackie Braun

And a new arrival from Raye Morgan
Keeping Her Baby's Secret
in September

Dear Reader,

It's an exciting year, as Harlequin is celebrating its sixtieth anniversary. So many years of wonderful books, and all those happy endings. In this day and age, who doesn't need that? I remember picking up my first Harlequin romance. It was years ago, when I was with my children at the library. While they were picking out their books, I went browsing through the paperback section and found Janet Dailey. Soon after, Nora Roberts became a favorite of mine, too. I've been hooked on romance ever since.

Even though I write for Harlequin now, I'm first and foremost an avid reader. Over the years we've all been lucky to be able to follow our favorite authors, book after book, year after year. I hope I've been one of them for you, too.

My latest book, *The Cowboy's Baby,* is a different kind of story. I wanted to write about a problem that resonates with a lot of young couples. My hero and heroine are married when the story opens… but they won't be for long. It isn't that Trace and Kira McKane don't love each other, but the complication of not being able to conceive a baby only adds to the strain of their failing ranch. Somewhere along the way they stopped talking, stopped turning to each other.

They need to get back the trust they lost. Could a baby help them save their crumbling marriage? What's so wonderful about a Harlequin Romance novel is that there will always be a happy ending.

Enjoy,

Patricia Thayer

PATRICIA THAYER

The Cowboy's Baby

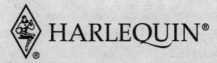

TORONTO • NEW YORK • LONDON
AMSTERDAM • PARIS • SYDNEY • HAMBURG
STOCKHOLM • ATHENS • TOKYO • MILAN • MADRID
PRAGUE • WARSAW • BUDAPEST • AUCKLAND

Recycling programs
for this product may
not exist in your area.

ISBN-13: 978-0-373-17595-6

THE COWBOY'S BABY

Originally published in the U.K. as HER BABY WISH.

First North American Publication 2009.

Copyright © 2009 by Patricia Wright.

www.eHarlequin.com

Printed in U.S.A.

Originally born and raised in Muncie, Indiana, **Patricia Thayer** is the second of eight children. She attended Ball State University, and soon afterward headed west. Over the years she's made frequent visits back to the Midwest, trying to keep up with her family's numerous weddings and births, but Patricia has called Orange County, California, home for many years. She not only enjoys the warm climate, but also the company and support of other published authors in the local writers' organization. For the past eighteen years she has had the unwavering support and encouragement of her critique group. It's a sisterhood like no other.

When not working on a story, Patricia can be found traveling the United States and Europe, taking in the scenery and doing story research while thoroughly enjoying herself, accompanied by Steve, her husband for over thirty-six years. Together they have three grown sons and three grandsons. Her own true-life heroes, as she calls them. On her rare days off from writing you might catch Patricia at Disneyland, spoiling those grandkids rotten! She also volunteers for the Grandparent Autism Network.

Patricia has written for over twenty years and has authored over thirty books. She has been nominated for both the National Readers' Choice Award and the prestigious RITA® Award. Her book *Nothing Short of a Miracle* won a *Romantic Times BOOKreviews* Reviewers' Choice award. She has been a guest reader at elementary schools and has lectured aspiring authors. A longtime member of Romance Writers of America, she has served as president and has held many other board positions for her local chapter in Orange County. She's a firm believer in giving back.

Check her Web site at www.patriciathayer.com for upcoming books.

To all the couples
who know the struggles and pain of infertility.
I pray you all will be blessed some day.
And a special congratulations to Michelle and Rod.

CHAPTER ONE

"I NEED you to come back home."

Trace McKane's grip tightened on the pitchfork as he spread fresh straw around Black Thunder's stall. He'd waited two long months to hear his wife say those words. The only problem was she didn't exactly sound sincere, and too many harsh words had passed between them to repair the damage so casually.

"I can't see how that's going to change anything." He continued to cover the floor as if Kira's presence hadn't affected him at all. But it had. He'd give up the family's Colorado ranch to have things back like they were before their problems started. And from the look of things lately, that might not be too far from the truth.

"Trace, please, just hear me out," she said.

He stopped his chores and finally looked at her. "Why, Kira? Haven't we said enough?" He straightened and tipped his hat back off his forehead. This was the first time he'd chanced a close up look at his wife since he'd moved out. She'd kept her distance, and so had he.

She placed her hands on her hips. "Oh, you made

your feelings perfectly clear. Things got rough so you walked out, without even trying to work things out."

"We were getting nowhere."

Kira Hyatt McKane was a natural beauty with curly wheat-blond hair that hung to her shoulders. She had an oval face, with a scattering of freckles across a straight nose and full, pouty lips. Her large brown eyes locked with his, causing his pulse to shoot into overdrive.

He wasn't going to take the bait and fight with her. "It's better I moved into the bunkhouse," he told her. He hated that they couldn't make their marriage work.

Yeah, he'd been running away. He'd spent a lot of time moving the herd to a higher pasture for the approaching summer. Many of those nights he'd slept under the stars, anything to keep from facing his lonely bunk. To keep from thinking about how he couldn't—no matter how much he loved Kira—make his marriage work.

"We both needed a breather."

God knew he'd missed her. The torture went on as his gaze moved over her navy T-shirt and the faded jeans that hugged her curves. Shapely hips and legs that he'd touched and caressed so often that he knew where every freckle was hidden. He also knew exactly where to touch to bring her pleasure.

He glanced away. Don't go there. That was past history. Their future together was bleak. He never thought he was a greedy man. He'd only wanted a traditional marriage; a wife to come home to and children to carry on the legacy of the ranch.

That had been when the trouble started, when their

marriage began to crumble and he couldn't do anything to stop it.

"Spring is a busy time," he told her. Especially this year since he had that payment due to his half brother, Jarrett. And it didn't look like there was much chance he could come up with the money.

Kira shook her head. "I know, Trace." She sighed. "And turning away from our problems doesn't help."

He cursed. "Yes, Kira, we have problems, but face it, lately we've been unable to come to terms with things. And I'm tired of beating my head against a wall." When he saw tears form in her eyes, he wanted to kick himself.

"I never meant for it to be this way."

He shrugged. The last thing he wanted was to argue. In the months before their separation that was all they'd done. Then they'd stopped talking altogether. What broke his heart was knowing he hadn't been able to give her what she needed.

"I just wanted us to be a real family," she added in a whispered voice.

"You had a funny way of showing it." He'd needed her to stand by him, and help him with his struggles with the ranch, but she was obsessed with her own problems.

Her eyes filled with tears. "There might have been a solution to help us both."

How many times had they tried? Even counseling, with some stranger listening to every way he'd failed his wife. He'd done about everything he could think of to make their marriage work. "How? More counseling?"

Kira shook her head. "I never should have asked you to go to counseling. I'm the one who's got the problem," she said, her voice husky with emotion. "I'm the one who needs to deal with things."

"As long as you feel that way, then you don't need me around."

Kira stepped closer and began to speak, but stopped. With a swallow, she tried again. "But, Trace, I do need you. I need you to stay with me another six months so I can have a baby, then you can have your divorce."

Trace glared at her. "What the hell?"

So finally she'd gotten his attention.

The first moment she'd seen Trace McKane, Kira knew for sure that he was the perfect man for her. That hadn't changed. Tall and lean, the handsome cowboy had gained his muscular build from years of working the McKane's Cattle Ranch. He had brown hair that always hung too long, brushing his shirt collar. His green-gray eyes were deep-set and when he looked at her she felt he could see into her soul. At first that had intrigued her, now it frightened her. The past months apart told her she didn't want to face a future without Trace. He was the one person she'd allowed to get close when she'd come to Winchester Ridge, Colorado, to take a guidance counselor job at the high school.

But there were some secrets she could never share… with anyone.

Now it was too late to do anything to save their marriage. "We received a letter today," she said, pulling the folded envelope out of her pocket. "It's from the adoption agency." Her voice trembled. "We've passed another screening for a baby."

Trace's eyes narrowed, then he threw his head back and laughed. "It's a joke, right?"

She didn't expect this reaction. "No."

"So for months we've been giving everyone the impression that we're the perfect couple and acceptable parents. Then we break up and we get the okay."

Kira squared her shoulders and looked him in the eye.

"No one knows you moved out, and I don't want anyone to. Not yet. Not until we receive a baby."

He froze, his jaw clenched. "If you want the divorce so bad, then adopt as a single parent." He tossed the pitchfork against the railing and marched out of the stall.

Kira hurried after him. "Trace, wait. Just hear me out." His fast pace had her nearly running to keep up. "We'll both get what we want. I'll have a baby, and you'll be free to marry someone who can give you what you want…children."

He stopped abruptly. "You have everything figured out, don't you?"

She shrugged, trying to hide her pain, wishing he'd say he'd stay with her and together they'd raise the baby. "No, but I know you want your own children. I can't give you that."

His eyes flashed his pain. "Yeah, I wanted a child— with you. But it didn't happen, and I wasn't enough for you." Without waiting for another word, he started out of the barn, leaving her in shock.

"It wouldn't be enough for you, Trace," Rushing

after him, she caught up to him again on the small porch of the bunkhouse. "I loved you and our life together." She meant it. Her life on the ranch with Trace had been perfect. For a while. Then her dream had slowly unraveled. It seemed as if God were punishing her for her past. She didn't want Trace to be punished because of her. That's the reason she had to put an end to this.

She forced away the thought. "Trace, I have a chance for a child…maybe my only chance. You can remarry and have a dozen children. So if you could be happier without me, I'm willing to let you go."

Trace closed his eyes and gripped the wooden post. He didn't know if he could handle this again. Their marriage had gone through so much turmoil while they'd tried several procedures to be able to conceive a baby. Toward the end, he couldn't take the look on her face every time they failed, until finally, the pressure drove her from him. He might have been the one who'd moved out of the house, but emotionally Kira had left him long before that.

Now, after long weeks of separation, he'd become reconciled to losing her. Then her sudden appearance today made him ache with want and need. But she was here only because of her need for a child, and to end their marriage.

"Do you honestly think we can pull this off? The last words we spoke to each other weren't exactly loving."

"The pressure is off now," she said. "We just have to go through the motions of being a couple. I've accepted that I may never conceive a baby, but I can still have a child." She held out the letter. "The agency says we've met their requirements and we can move on to the next step."

How could he forget the classes, the long interviews, the background checks. They'd even been finger-printed. He glanced from the paper in her hand to the hopeful look on her face. He felt the familiar tug in his chest.

"They'll send someone out for a home study. To visit with us and see our home."

"So what do you want me to do? Play the loving husband?"

She rested her hand on his arm, her dark eyes pleading. "Would that be so hard?"

Damn, she didn't play fair and he had trouble denying her anything. "I don't think we can pull it off, Kira. Not where we are right now."

She paused. "It's only for about six months. That's how long it takes for the adoption to be final." She looked sad. "Is it that hard to pretend you love me?"

The next evening, seated at the kitchen table at the house, Kira tried to finish the end-of-the-year paper-work, but her mind kept wandering back to Trace.

"What else is new?" she grumbled as she got up and went to the coffeemaker. After refilling her mug, she walked to the window and stared out at the breathtak-ing view of the Roan Plateau. She'd come to love this place. So different from the busy streets of Denver.

Five years ago she'd come to Winchester Ridge to start a new life. With her new college degree in hand, she'd come to interview for a teaching position at the high school. She'd gotten the job and needed a place to live.

The town's real estate broker, Jarrett McKane, had shown her an apartment, then taken her to lunch. At the local café, they'd run into his younger brother, Trace.

It had been an instant attraction. After that she'd accepted a few more dates from Jarrett in the hope of running into Trace.

Finally two weeks later, the rugged rancher showed up at school and asked her out. It seemed like forever before he kissed her, but it had been well worth the wait. She closed her eyes, remembering his slow hands skimming over her, softly caressing her skin.

Trace's kisses were lethal. She remembered each touch of his lips against her heated flesh. How hungry he'd made her, stirring her desire. Suddenly warmth ran down her spine settling low in her stomach. Her eyes shot open as she groaned in frustration.

"Oh God," she whispered as she sank against the counter, her body aching. Never in her life had anyone made her feel the way Trace McKane had. After her parents' automobile accident and death, she'd been alone for a lot of years. She'd thought she'd finally found a home, a place where she could belong.

Yesterday, she'd wanted to beg Trace to come home, but her own pain and hurt prevented it. She knew the past few months she'd been horrible to live with. But how could any man understand the anguish she'd gone through, not just with the pain of her disease, but knowing she hadn't been able to conceive a baby?

She glanced back through the window, seeing the light on in the bunkhouse. "Oh, Trace, would you have loved me if you knew the truth about me?"

The past flooded back. She tried to push it away, but

it always hovered close enough to force her to remember, taking the brightness away from any happiness she tried to grasp. Maybe the guilt had been what drove her, caused her to keep pushing Trace away.

The familiar sadness blanketed her. With each passing month her fertility problems had loomed ever darker. With the endometriosis, her chances diminished daily until the day would come when she'd probably need more surgery to relieve her of the recurring scar tissue.

But with the passing of time, her dreams seemed to be fading anyway, along with her marriage.

The sound of the back door opening caught Kira's attention. Living this far out in the country, she knew it could only be Jonah Calhoun, the ranch foreman. Or Trace. Her heart raced as she waited, and her hopes were rewarded when her husband walked into the kitchen.

She tried to breathe but it was difficult. Trace McKane still affected her in the same way he had when she'd first met him. It was obvious he had just showered and put on a fresh shirt and jeans. Hope spread through her as she realized he might have done it for her.

"Hi," she managed. "Would you like a cup of coffee?"

He nodded. "I could use one." He walked to the counter and took the steaming mug she offered. Then Kira picked up her cup and started for the table.

"I thought caffeine was bad for your condition," he said.

She was touched that he remembered. "I usually don't drink it, but tonight I have work to finish. I need all the help I can get to stay alert."

"I guess school is getting out soon. So it looks like

it's going to be a busy time for both of us." He drank from his cup, then studied her. She felt the heat of his silver gaze spread over her, warming her. She hated they were talking so politely, when she desperately wanted him to take her into his arms and tell her he wanted to move back permanently to be her husband and father to her baby.

He glanced away. "Cal wants to know if you're still planning the senior roundup to be here this year."

She nodded. "I hope to. The kids have been talking about it for weeks. That is, if it's okay with you?"

He shrugged. "Not a problem. Cal just wants a head count so we'll know how many hands we need to hire."

Trace leaned against the counter, trying to relax. Impossible. Since his dad's death three years ago, he'd had to run the cattle operation mostly on his own.

"Do you have a date set for the roundup?" she asked.

"In two weeks."

She nodded. "That's perfect. Graduation will be over, so we don't have to worry about interrupting study time."

Trace hated the silence lingering between them. What he hated most of all was feeling like a stranger in his own house, a stranger to his wife.

"Have you given any thought to what we talked about?" she finally asked him.

"It's kind of hard not to." He shifted his weight trying to ease the tightness in his chest. "You tell a man you want to adopt a child, and in the same breath give him his walking papers."

"I'm sorry, Trace. I never wanted it to turn out this way. But in the end it might be best for both of us."

He heard the tears in her voice. "Is it really that easy,

Kira? Well, it's not for me. If I agree I also sign papers for this child. I'm responsible for him or her, too."

"Trace, I know I'm asking a lot."

"No, you don't," he interrupted her. "You're asking me to move back into the house and take responsibility for a child, then just to walk away."

She wanted more, so much more from him. But she couldn't ask for another chance. "I don't expect to have things be like they once were. Yes, we have to live in the same house, but if we're lucky enough to get a baby, I'll handle all the child's needs. I won't ask for any help."

He was silent for a long time. "And after the six months, I sign away all rights to the child."

He made it sound so calculating. She managed a nod.

He cursed and turned away.

"Please, Trace, I'm afraid if we tell the agency we're not together now, then later, I'll have to start from the beginning as a single parent."

He drove his fingers through his hair. "I'm not sure I can do this, Kira."

She bit down on her lower lip. "Please, I want this opportunity, Trace. It might be my last chance."

Trace fought to control his anger. It had always been about a baby. What about them? Why couldn't she offer to work out their problems? Instead of wanting to push him aside when he wasn't needed any more.

"Trace, I don't magically expect us to return to our roles of husband and wife. I'll move into the guest room and you can have your bedroom back."

This was all so crazy. Trace wasn't sure if he could resist Kira, living under the same roof. If he moved back into the house now, it'd be damn difficult to resist going to her bed.

He placed his coffee mug in the sink, then went to her, bracing his hands on either side of her. He stared into those honey-brown eyes, knowing there were secrets hidden in their depths. Secrets she wouldn't share with anyone, not even with him. "You talk about this situation like it's a business transaction. I have my doubts about us being able to pull this off."

She swallowed hard, but didn't speak.

His attention went to her mouth, tempting him like no woman ever had. His heart raced and his gut tightened. He ached to taste her, to stir up those feelings that made him crazy with need. It had been so long.

"Trace." Her voice was a throaty whisper as her hand came up to his face. "Can't we try?"

Her sultry voice swept over him like a caress. He closed his eyes, picturing her in their bed, willing and wanton, welcoming his kisses, his touches as he moved over her heated body.

"Damn you, Kira." His mouth closed over hers in a hungry kiss. She wrapped her arms around his neck as he jerked her against his body already hard with desire. Her mouth opened on a sigh, and he dove inside to taste her. He moved against her, hungry for the contact. It wasn't enough, he needed all of her.

But Kira couldn't give it to him. Would they ever be able to be what the other needed?

He broke off the kiss and stepped back. "I've got to go." He headed to the door only to have her call to him.

He didn't turn around, knowing he'd weaken to her request. "Kira, I need more time."

"Please, Trace." She hesitated. "Just keep up the pretense that we're married until you decide what to do."

In his heart Trace would always be married to Kira. He'd loved her since the moment he laid eyes on her. That hadn't changed. But could he hang around and watch their marriage die a slow agonizing death?

He faced her. "So you expect me live in limbo until the adoption goes through?" The words stuck in his throat.

She blinked, looking surprised. "No. I'm asking if you would give it six months until they give us permanent custody. After that I won't try to hold you, or make you responsible for the child. I'll move into town and not ask anything more of you. As soon as I get another counseling job, I'll move away."

Damn, there it was. She couldn't say it any plainer. The chant rang repeatedly in his head. *She only wants a child.* "You're asking a lot, Kira."

"I know," was all she said in her defense.

"What do I get out of this deal? What are you willing to give me?"

She blinked at his question, but soon recovered. Her arms tightened around his neck. "What do you want, Trace? If it was me, all you had to do any time was walk through that door. I've been here the whole time, wanting you."

His body stirred at the feel of her length pressed against him. The easy way would be to give them what they both wanted. He wasn't sure he could, knowing in the end he could lose everything anyway. Everything. Not only would he give up Kira, but a child.

"Like I said, I'll have to think about it." He removed her hands, and walked out before he changed his mind. Before he did something crazy like agreeing to her request.

CHAPTER TWO

OF ALL mornings to oversleep.

Kira pulled her leather satchel from the back seat, slammed the car door and rushed off across the parking lot toward the large brick building, Winchester Ridge High School. And the nine o'clock meeting.

After Trace had left the house, she hadn't been able to finish her work until well after midnight. Then she lay awake a long time, reliving her husband's visit, their kiss.

Trace's familiar taste. The way he held her, reminding her how well their bodies meshed together. She delighted in the fact she could still make his control slip, just as hers had. She had to stop herself from trying to convince him to stay and make love to her.

Oh God, it had been a long time since Trace had touched her.

"Mrs. McKane, are you all right?"

Kira shook away the fantasy and glanced at her student, Jody Campbell. "Oh, Jody. Yes, I'm fine. Just a lot of things on my mind." She picked up her pace toward the counselors' office, realizing the student was staying right with her. "What are you doing out of class?"

"Mr. Douglas let me leave early because I needed to see you." The pretty girl hesitated. "It's about volunteer time at the retirement home. All the kids voted it as our class project, but some don't have enough hours to come to the senior roundup."

"Give me the list and I'll talk to them," Kira said as she stopped at the counseling department's door and took the paper.

Seeing Jody reminded her that she'd gotten a notice from her English teacher. The promising student's work had been suffering the past month. Kira hated that her own personal distractions had caused her to neglect one of the best students in the senior class.

"Why don't you come back at three o'clock? We should talk."

Jody hesitated again. "I work at four so I need to catch the three-thirty bus."

She couldn't let this slip any longer, not with finals next week. "Well, I could give you a lift if you like and we can have a quick chat."

Her once-enthusiastic student kept her eyes cast down. "Okay."

Kira signed Jody's pass and sent her off to class just as the bell rang. She walked inside the guidance office and into the first glass cubicle. She hated being distracted from her work. And these last few weeks, it had been especially difficult for her to keep focused on a job she was crazy about. She loved doing extra things to stay involved with the teenagers.

Kira was the sponsor for this year's senior class, including all activities. Doing service hours and giving back to the community was an important part of their curriculum. It helped to develop their social skills, and it looked good on their college applications. She rewarded those students with senior roundup at McKane Ranch.

Winchester Ridge was a small ranching town, but the teenagers loved to spend the day helping with the roundup and branding. Followed by a barbecue and barn dance that closed out their senior year with wonderful memories.

Kira sank into her desk chair. Not all kids were that lucky. Suddenly the last fifteen years faded away as her thoughts went back to her own high school days. Shy and naive, she'd been passed around to so many different foster homes it had been difficult to make friends. So when someone gave her attention, she'd been eager for it, and easy to be taken advantage of. Those lonely years had been a big motivator for her career choice.

At the sound of the knock on her door, Kira looked up to see her fellow counselor and friend, Michelle Turner, peer in.

"Michele," she greeted. "Are you coming for the meeting?"

"It's been postponed until one o'clock," her friend said as she walked inside the small enclosure and closed the door. "Kira, are you all right?"

She gave her friend a bright smile. "I'm fine."

The young teacher sat down in the only other chair. "No, you're not."

Kira shook her head. Michele had been the one person she'd confided in about her inability to conceive. The fellow teacher had been her first friend when she'd come to the western Colorado town. "No, really. We've gotten word from the adoption agency."

Michele's pretty blue eyes lit up. "Oh, that's great news." She frowned. "Why so sad?"

Kira shrugged. "Hormones, probably. And Trace. He's a little hesitant about the idea."

Michele leaned forward. "You two have been through a lot over this and now that you're so close to having a baby, he's probably a little scared."

And he wants his own child, Kira added silently. "It's more." She looked her friend in the eye, knowing she'd never betray her confidence. "It hasn't been easy living with me this last year."

"You've gone through a lot, trying to have a baby."

Kira released a shuttering breath. "Trace moved out to the bunkhouse two months ago."

"Oh, Kira." Michele shook her head. "Isn't that just like a man? When they can't deal with things, they up and leave. Well, I know Trace loves you."

And Kira wasn't so sure of that anymore. "I might have pushed him too far this time. We both said things that can't be taken back." She recalled the hurtful words she'd thrown at him. And yesterday she mentioned the "D" word. It was all or nothing now.

"Then march out to that bunkhouse and convince him to come back home."

"I'm not sure that will work."

"How do you know if you don't try? So go and seduce your husband." Michele glanced at her watch. "I've got to get back. Can we do lunch later in the week?"

"Sure. Are you going to help chaperone at the round-up?"

Michele grinned. "I wouldn't miss it. Is your good-looking brother-in-law going to be there?"

Kira was surprised by her friend's interest in Jarrett. "I'm not sure."

Michelle waved off the question then hugged her. "I'll see you later." She walked out.

Kira leaned back in her chair. Could she get Trace to come back home, and get him to change his mind about the divorce? Could they work together to repair their mess of a marriage?

She thought back to the last time Trace had wanted to be close to her. In the weeks before he'd moved out, her once-loving husband hadn't wanted to touch her, or even be in the same house with her. And she couldn't blame him. The sad part was she'd driven him out. Out of his own home.

Trace loved the McKane Ranch, one of the oldest in the area. He was a cattleman like his father and grandfather before him. There had been times when she was a little jealous of his dedication, maybe if he'd talk about the operation with her it would help. Even when he'd bought out part of his brother's land, she hadn't been asked anything about it until it came time to sign the loan papers. She just wanted to feel like a part of his dreams.

Kira felt her chest tighten with the familiar ache. The same feeling she'd had when she'd lost her parents in the accident and her grandmother wouldn't take her into her home. *Rejection.* When she had to go into foster care, then from home to home. *Rejection.* When she fell in love with the first boy who gave her the time of day, he'd abandoned her, too. *Rejection.* Now, her marriage…

Kira sat up straighter. Why was she thinking so much about the past? She'd worked so hard to put those years behind her. A glance at the calendar gave her the answer. It was approaching the seventh of June. Fifteen years had passed and it still hurt like a fresh wound.

No! This baby was going to change things. She was going to have her family, even if it was only part of one.

"Kira…"

She turned around to see Trace at the door. He was dressed in his usual jeans and Western shirt, his cowboy hat in his hand. With her heart pounding, she stood.

"Trace." He never came to her school. "Is something wrong?"

"Do you have some time to talk?"

"Sure." She stepped aside. "Come in."

He glanced around the busy office. "I'd rather go somewhere else. Can you leave for a while?"

She checked her watch. "I'm free for the next hour."

"Let's go for some coffee."

"Sure." Kira grabbed her purse, stepped out into the hall and together they walked out of the building. When Trace placed his hand against the small of her back, she shivered.

"Are you okay?" he asked.

"Yes," she lied. "I'm fine. I just need some coffee."

He gave her a sideways glance. "You should switch to decaf."

She studied his profile. Trace McKane had always been serious by nature. He didn't smile easily, but when he did he was irresistible.

They were quiet as he helped her to his truck, then drove past all the recently built, chain restaurants to the older section of Winchester Ridge to Bonnie's Diner. Still a favorite with the locals.

They took a booth by the picture window. The red vinyl seats were worn and cracked, repaired by tape over the years. The place was clean and the food good. Right now, there weren't any customers, only the sound of a country ballad coming from the old fifties-style jukebox.

Trace signaled the waitress for two coffees and sat down across from Kira. He wondered if he should have waited until she got home to talk with her.

After what happened between them last night, he should be staying away from her, completely. But here he was, sitting across from her. Just looking at her had him working to breathe normally. Nothing had changed. Kira Hyatt had gotten to him from the moment he laid eyes on her, right here in this diner. It had been the only time he'd ever won out against his older sibling. For once Jarrett hadn't gotten the girl. Younger brother, Trace had.

But Trace had nothing now. Not a wife. Not a marriage. It helped to remember the bad times. That kept him from storming back into the house they'd shared for five years. To a life he'd thought was perfect, but reality hit and he'd learned nothing was perfect. That it hit home again as he recalled that Kira only wanted a six-month marriage.

The waitress placed their mugs on the table. The older woman, Alice Burns, gave them a warm smile. She'd worked here for as long as he could remember. "Well, how are Mr. and Mrs. McKane doin' today?"

"Just fine, Alice," Trace answered.

"How's your granddaughter?" Kira asked.

The fifty-something woman grinned. "Best not get me started on little Emily. But she's gonna have to share me soon because Carol's pregnant again. A boy this time."

Kira's smile froze. "That's wonderful. Congrat-ulations."

Alice eyed the couple. "You two should think about having a few yourselves." Before they could answer, the waitress walked away.

Trace watched Kira fight her emotions as she took a drink.

"Alice didn't know, Kira," Trace said.

"I know that." Kira wrapped a strand of golden-blond hair behind her ear, leaving the wispy bangs along her forehead. "Why did you need to see me?"

Okay this was all business. "A woman from the adoption agency called after you left."

Her brown eyes widened. "So soon. What did she say?"

"I didn't get to talk to her. Just a message on the machine. It just said that she'd call back again."

"Darn, I wonder if she'll call the office." She glanced at him. "Did she leave a number where I could reach her?"

It hurt when she used the word "I" and not "we". He pulled the paper from his pocket and slid it across the table. "I don't think you should call her just yet."

She looked hurt. "But I have to."

"What are you going to tell her, Kira?"

She blinked at him. "We're just talking to her, Trace. I don't want to delay the process, it takes a long time. We're probably just going to be put on a waiting list."

"I still have to pretend we're married."

"You are married—to me." She lost her attitude. "But as I told you the baby will be my responsibility."

So she hadn't changed her mind. He was to do

nothing concerning the child. "We aren't even living under the same roof."

"I never asked you to move out in the first place."

"You know why I did, Kira. We were headed for disaster." He'd hated leaving, and if she'd asked him to stay just once, he would have in a heartbeat. Now, it was too late.

She sighed. "Please, just listen to what Mrs. Fletcher has to say, that's all I ask."

"Okay, I'll talk with the woman. See what she has to say."

"Really?" Tears flooded her eyes. "Oh, Trace, thank you."

He raised a hand. "Don't thank me, yet. I'll agree to another home visit. Afterward we'll see where we go from there. I can't commit to anything more."

She nodded. "Does that mean you're moving back to the house?"

Before Trace could come up with an answer they were interrupted.

"Well, look who's wandered in off the range."

They both glanced up to see Jarrett McKane standing at their table. He was tall, athletic and good-looking. He knew it, too. Jarrett knew a lot of things, all you had to do was ask him.

Trace straightened. He didn't want his half brother here. Not now. "Hello, Jarrett."

"Trace." His brother turned to Kira. "Hello, pretty sister-in-law."

Kira smiled. "Hi, Jarrett."

Grabbing a chair, he turned it around and straddled it. He glanced between the two of them. "You two look serious. There wouldn't be trouble in paradise, would there? Kira, you just let me know if this guy isn't treating you right and I'll knock some sense into him."

Kira shifted in her seat as she continued to smile at her brother-in-law. "Everything is fine, Jarrett, but thanks for asking."

At their first meeting when Kira arrived in town, Jarrett had laid on his easy chair but it hadn't taken her long to realize that Jarrett McKane was out for himself. He was attentive to his women though, but that was another problem, there were a lot of women.

Both brothers were handsome, but Jarrett had been the school sports hero and a college graduate. Meanwhile Trace had stayed and worked on the ranch with his father, going to college locally.

"Anytime." He looked at Trace. "I need to talk to you about our arrangement. Could you come to my office?"

"Later. Kira and I are talking right now."

"Seems like you could do that at home. Hell, you sleep in the same bed." There was a wicked look in Jarrett's eyes. "That's right. It's branding time so you sleep out with your calves." He winked at Kira. "Makes for a lonely wife left at home."

"And sometimes I sleep out with the calves, too," Kira said, worried things might come to blows.

The brothers had never been close. Jarrett had been six years old when his mother died, and his father, John, remarried Claire, and a year later she had given birth to Trace. The distance had grown when their parents retired and moved to a warmer climate in Arizona. Now, both parents had passed away.

"My brother's a lucky man to have you. Although I

tried my best, he won you fair and square." He winked at Kira. "But it's still a long way to go before the score is even, bro."

Later that afternoon, Trace rode toward the barn. After returning from town, he'd saddled up Thunder and went out to check the herd. He'd wasted the morning already when he needed to finish things before the roundup.

He rotated his tired shoulders, felt his eyes burn, a sure sign that lack of sleep had taken a toll on him. And confronting his brother hadn't exactly made his day. He'd wanted to spend more time with Kira, but they hadn't managed that, either. So far, they'd talked very little of what was most important to him: their marriage.

Trace climbed off his horse and walked him into the barn. The immaculately clean structure had been the result of too much time on his hands. Since moving to the bunkhouse, he'd tried to stay busy, and his already organized barn had gotten a complete sweep, with every piece of tack on the property being cleaned or polished.

It had been his sleep time that suffered. Even his fatigue hadn't helped him on those long nights. He walked his stallion into the stall, removed the saddle and carried it to the tack room. On his way out, he ran into his foreman, Cal.

"Hey, Trace. What's up?"

"You tell me, Cal," he said. "How many men have you got for the roundup?"

The forty-one-year-old foreman, Jonah Calhoun, took off his hat and scratched his gray-streaked brown hair. A single man, he'd worked for the McKane Ranch for years, and was also Trace's friend. "Besides our two part-time hands, another half a dozen like you asked. I also ran into Joel and Hal Lewis at the feed store. They're willing to come and help out, too, as long as we can give them a hand next month."

Trace nodded. "Can do. I'll give them a call."

Together, they walked back to Thunder's stall. Trace removed the horse's bridle and blanket, then took the brush and began grooming him.

Cal snapped his fingers. "Oh, I forgot, your brother stopped by earlier, looking for you."

Trace didn't like Jarrett dogging him. "He found me at the diner."

Cal frowned. "I thought you went to see Kira."

Trace nodded. "We went for coffee."

The foreman smiled. "Good idea, take her to the place where you two met."

"I just wanted to talk to her. Alone."

The smile grew bigger. "Get anything settled?" Then he raised his hand. "Sorry, Trace, that's none of my business. I'm just glad you two got together."

Trace continued to stroke the animal. "We were talking until Jarrett showed up."

The foreman's eyes narrowed. "He seemed bent on seeing you. What's he up to?"

Cal knew as well as Trace that Jarrett never did anything unless it benefited him. "He probably wants to know when that last payment I owe him is coming."

The foreman frowned. He knew the conditions of the loan. "Are you late?"

Trace shook his head. "No, but I'm not sure I can make the full amount on the final payment." He could lose it all.

"Would your brother give you more time? I mean, with the market the way it is."

"I doubt it. When has he ever done me a favor?"

Five years ago, Jarrett couldn't wait to sell off most of his share of the ranch, and offered Trace the first opportunity to buy it. Trace hadn't hesitated, but things had been tight this past year, and the payment was due to Jarrett in thirty days.

"I might have to sell the breeding bulls."

"No way. You need another year or two to build the herd. There's some serious money in those guys. Rocky will sire some good stock."

Trace put down the brush. "But I can get ready cash for them. Joel Lewis is interested. And I can't lose everything now." His thoughts turned to Kira. He could lose more than the ranch.

"You know Lewis is mostly talk. Look, Trace, I have some money saved I could loan you."

Trace was touched by the offer. "Thanks, Cal, I'm grateful for the offer, but it's not a good idea to borrow from friends."

"Maybe I want to invest if Jarrett is threatening you. Not a full partnership, but just a percentage of the place." Kind light-blue eyes studied Trace. "Well, maybe you can talk it over with Kira before you nix the idea."

Trace walked out of the stall. "She's never shown much interest in the running of the ranch."

"Maybe she would this time."

Trace pushed his hat back and sighed. He didn't want to add to their troubles. "She has enough on her mind."

Cal nodded. "If you say so. Well, I guess I better go put away the feed that was delivered."

Trace stopped him. "Has Kira said something to you?"

"No. She just always asks about things, and seems genuinely interested when I tell her." The foreman shrugged. "But I can't tell you how to talk to your wife, Trace."

He hadn't been talking to Kira at all until she'd come to see him yesterday. And she wasn't going to be his wife much longer. "Hell, I've been living in the bunkhouse for the past two months. I haven't been doing such a great job of it myself."

"And you don't need a lecture from me. But I think if there are problems with the missus, living out here and keeping things from her isn't the best way for fixin' things between you."

Cal was probably the only one who knew about their problems. "The adoption agency notified us. Kira wants me to move back to the house and pretend we're a happy couple."

A smile appeared on his friend's face. "You don't look very happy about it."

"All she wants is six months. After the adoption becomes final she's going to leave."

Cal raised an eyebrow then he said, "I know it's been rough. Kira's gone through a lot and she wants a baby."

"So do I. And how can I just walk away from a child?"

"Who says you have to? You can still be the kid's father, Kira's husband. Who's to say you can't get an extension on the six months?"

So much had already passed between them, so much hurt. He didn't know if they could go back to how it was before. "I don't know if I can."

"If you're not ready, then take it slow."

Trace never had been one who shared things, but Cal was as close as they came. He valued his opinion, and advice. "She wants me to stay in the house but not in the same room."

His friend smiled slowly. "Hey, it's a start."

"Trace?"

At the sound of Kira's voice, he turned to find her standing in the barn entrance, holding a bag of groceries.

"Kira." He walked toward her and took the sack from her. "Is there a problem?" Great, is that all he could come up with?

She glanced away shyly. "I had an easy afternoon at school and decided to cook supper." She looked at Cal and smiled. "Hello, Jonah."

"Kira, it's nice to see you."

"It's nice to see you, too. I hope you're ready for about thirty teenagers coming out."

"Are we ever ready?"

Kira laughed. "I guess not, but it's fun."

Trace found he was jealous of their easy banter. "Is there a reason you came to see me?"

Kira looked at him. "I wanted to ask if you'd come to supper." She turned back to Cal. "You're welcome, too, Jonah."

The foreman blushed. "Thank you for the invitation, Kira, but it's my bowling night." He tipped his hat. "I should finish up my chores." He leaned toward his friend and whispered, "Slow and easy." Cal turned and walked out.

"What did he say?" Kira asked.

He shrugged. "Just something I need to remember."

An hour later when Trace stepped inside the house, the scent of apples and cinnamon teased his nose. Ordinarily he didn't take time to look around; he'd grown up in this house, but today he was mindful of it all.

A wide staircase led to a second floor where there were four large bedrooms. The living room was painted gray-green to offset the dark woodwork and floors. An overstuffed green sofa faced the used-brick fireplace.

That was when he noticed them, Kira's touches. An easy chair she'd bought for him right after they were married, saying he needed a place to relax. The large coffee table where the photo album of his childhood rested. More family pictures hung on the brightly painted walls. His family, not hers. He remembered her saying she lost her parents' pictures while moving around in foster care. He'd never thought much about her being alone in her life. She'd always seemed so outgoing and everyone liked her.

Trace moved quickly down the hall through the dining room, which was a sunny-gold color trimmed in oak wainscoting. The scent of lemon oil rose from the long, drop-leaf oak table and eight high-back chairs that had also belonged to his parents. He entered the kitchen, the one room that he and Kira had changed. And it had needed it. Everything had been out-of-date, from the appliances to the cupboards. Just a few months after their small wedding, the room had been gutted and everything was replaced.

A bowl of red apples sat on the round maple table. Everything looked the same, but it wasn't. He wanted desperately to push time back to when everything was perfect in his marriage.

He found Kira at the counter, taking pieces of chicken from the skillet. She glanced over her shoulder and smiled. "Hi."

He had trouble finding the words. "Hi. Am I too early?"

"No. Just in time."

His gaze combed over her. He was starved for her. Denying himself the pleasure she could give him had been punishing. Today she had on one of her prim schoolteacher blouses, his favorite, a rose-pink one that brought out the color of her skin.

He swallowed back the dryness in his throat. "How did school go today?"

"Fine," she said. "Everyone is complaining about finals."

He leaned against the counter. He'd missed talking with her. "I remember that age, it seemed to take an eternity to get to the end of school."

She smiled and started setting out the food. "The seniors are anxious to graduate, and get me out of their hair."

He knew that wasn't true. They all loved her. The girls considered her a friend, and the boys were half in love with her. She was young, barely thirty-one, and attractive. They all gravitated to her. "And a lot are going to be heartbroken at saying goodbye to you."

"What does that mean?"

"You've always given your students a lot of attention."

"And that's a bad thing?"

"No, it just means you're dedicated, and very good
at what you do. Not to mention pretty."

Kira couldn't believe she was blushing at her
husband's compliment. Trace had told her she was
attractive before, but not for a long time. He hadn't
talked to her at all.

"Thank you," she said.

He shrugged. "I'm not saying anything that isn't
true."

"It's still nice to hear," she said. They looked at each
other for a long time. Kira tried not to react, but it was
impossible. Trace McKane was a handsome man. She'd
thought that the first time she'd seen him. She'd been
in town less than twenty-four hours before falling hope-
lessly in love. Something she'd never thought would
happen, but the quiet rancher somehow convinced her
to trust again. His slow hands and eager mouth coaxed
her into giving herself to him, and they married within
two months. From that first night of loving to now,
she'd never regretted that decision.

She turned and opened the refrigerator to get the milk.
The cool air felt good against her heated face. She couldn't
believe how nervous she was acting. He was her husband,
for God's sake. No, Trace hadn't been her husband for
weeks. And sadly that wasn't going to change.

CHAPTER THREE

AN HOUR later, Kira sat at the kitchen table and watched as Trace finished the last of his meal.

He leaned back in the chair. "That was delicious, Kira."

She let out a breath, not realizing she'd been holding it. "I'm glad you liked it."

He gave a half smile. "Can't deny I've always loved your fried chicken."

And she loved his praise. "I shouldn't fix it. It isn't exactly healthy, especially the gravy."

"Once in a while won't hurt me."

It definitely hadn't hurt his waistline, she thought, visualizing the six-pack abs hidden under his shirt. She nodded and started to get up. "Coffee?"

He touched her hand to stop her and she felt a sudden jolt. "I'll get it," he said.

Kira relented, but her hungry gaze followed Trace to the coffeemaker. He stood nearly six-feet-two-inches tall, and since she was nearly five-nine, she loved his height. Her attention moved over a Western shirt that outlined his broad shoulders and narrow waist. She loved that long, lean look, especially when he wore Wrangler jeans.

And nothing else.

Heat suddenly swarmed her body just as Trace turned around. He gave her a curious look, but remained silent as he walked back to the table. He set down the mugs and she noticed his hands. Memories flooded her head, as she recalled his firm, but gentle touches, how he stroked her, bringing her pleasure.

He took a seat across from her. "I'm glad to see you've taken my advice and are on the decaf."

She sat up straighter. "I realized I need more sleep."

"We could all use a little more of that." His gaze locked with hers. "Though I doubt I can blame my problem on the caffeine."

Kira swallowed hard. She wanted to explore his comment further, but couldn't. They had another topic that needed attention. "I called Mrs. Fletcher at the agency," she said in a rush.

Trace didn't look surprised. "I figured you would." He set down his mug. "What did she have to say?"

"She wants to come for another home visit the first of next week."

Trace took a sip of coffee, then asked, "What did you tell her?"

"That I'd check with you, but Monday seemed okay for us." Kira held her breath, waiting, praying that Trace would agree to this.

"What are we going to say to her when she gets here?"

She hesitated, feeling her heart pounding. "That we want a baby."

Trace met Kira's anxious gaze. He could see how much she wanted this. There had been a lot of disappointment in the past two years for both of them. She'd gone through so much, both physically and emotionally, trying to get pregnant.

His own excitement began to build. A family with Kira. Was it still possible?

He wanted to make their marriage work, but her need for a child had become an obsession, leaving no room for them. By the time he moved out, she seemed relieved he was gone. Once she got her child would she turn her attention back to them? Either way he couldn't deny her.

"I'll be around Monday."

Those big brown eyes widened. "Really? Oh, Trace."

She jumped out of her chair, threw her arms around his neck and hugged him. Trace reached for her, gripping her by the waist so they both wouldn't topple over.

Kira ended up on his lap and when she pulled back there were tears in her eyes. "Thank you," she whispered.

He couldn't resist, and brushed away a tear off her cheek. Seeing her rich brown eyes staring back at his caused his blood to stir. It always had, but he couldn't let it happen, not after all the pain they'd caused each other.

He stood her on her feet. He got up, too, then backed away but ran into the counter. "You don't have to thank me. We'd always planned on children. I haven't agree to everything."

She refused to look away. "Under the circumstances…and reasons you've agreed to do this, I still thank you."

The hard ache in his body told him he was crazy to be this close to Kira. "Like you said it's a long waiting list." He drew a breath and inhaled that soft, womanly scent that was only her.

"Well, you've made me very happy." She leaned forward and placed a tender kiss on his mouth. He sucked in a breath as another jolt of desire shot through him. "And I promise I'll give you what you want."

"That'd be a first time in a long time," he murmured, trying to guard against his weakness for her.

"You know what I mean," she added. "You're doing this for me, I promise when it's over, I won't contest anything."

What had happened to them? At one time, he'd wanted to give her everything. They'd planned a lifetime together. Now, she wanted nothing from him, especially not his love.

"I should go," he told her, not wanting the conversation to go sour if they brought up any more of the past hurt. "I need to go check on that bad section of fence. I don't want Rocky to wander off," he rambled on. He stole another look at her and his pulse accelerated, weighing down each step he took.

"We still have things to talk about," Kira called to him. "Maybe after I'm home from school tomorrow."

Trace nodded, then headed for the back door, praying she wouldn't stop him. He worked to remember the misery they'd caused each other during their last months together. He hurried out into the cool night, and it felt good against his heated skin, but even jumping into a pool of ice water wouldn't cool off his need for Kira.

He doubted anything would, ever. That still didn't give him any hope that they were meant to be together.

The next morning, Kira had renewed hope that things were going to work out. She knew she needed to take things slow with Trace. He never rushed into anything.

She walked into her office to find Jody waiting for her. When Kira had driven the girl to her job yesterday, there wasn't much time to talk about anything except plans for the senior roundup. That was why Kira had set up this morning's meeting.

Jody stood. "Hello, Mrs. McKane."

"Good morning, Jody." Kira unlocked her office, went inside and set her things on her desk. After putting her purse in the bottom drawer, she motioned to Jody to take a seat, then she did the same.

"Okay, Jody, there are no distractions now." She worked up a smile. "It's just you and me." She took the file from her in-box and opened it. "I've talked with your teachers, Mr. Franklin and Miss Meehan, who informed me your grades have dropped considerably as of late. Jody, is there something going on, has something happened?"

The young girl looked pale, almost sickly. Her blond hair was long, but it looked unkempt today. She wasn't wearing any makeup, not even lip gloss. So different from the impeccably groomed girl Kira had known. Jody looked tired, no exhausted. Then it started adding up, the bad grades, and the sudden breakup with her boyfriend. Could Jody be pregnant?

Kira's heart sank as she worked hard not to look down at the girl's waistline. "I know I'm your guidance counselor, but I hope after our four years together, I'm your friend, too."

The student glanced away and shrugged. "I know you've helped me so much." She hesitated. "It's just… it's hard to talk about."

Jody Campbell lived with her single mother, and money was always tight. With Jody's high grade point average, Kira had been working tirelessly to help her get scholarships and financial aid for college.

"Jody, two months ago you were excited about going away to college. Has something changed that?"

She drew an unsteady breath and nodded. "Ben and I broke up." Tears filled her eyes. "He signed up to go into the Army."

"I'm sorry, Jody." Ben Kerrigan was another senior. The two had been dating for the past few months. She could see the girl's heartbreak. "When does he have to leave?"

A tear rolled down the girl's cheek. "The end of June. He said he won't have time for me, and doesn't even want to write me, or anything. He said it's better this way." The girl broke down and sobbed.

Kira reached for Jody and hugged her close. "I'm so sorry."

She knew too well how much teenage romance hurt. And in some cases you never lost the scars. Her thoughts went back nearly sixteen years earlier to her first love, Mike Purcell. Mike had broken more than her heart—he'd nearly destroyed her when he hadn't stood by her. That painful time still lingered in her memory. She had never shared it with anyone, not even Trace.

She blinked away her own tears and pulled back. "Jody. Listen to me. If you need me, for anything, I'm here."

The girl nodded, taking the tissue from Kira. "It's too late," she whispered.

"No, it's not. Unless you're changing your mind about college?"

The girl glanced away. "It would be hard for my mom if I go away. She depends on me."

Mrs. Campbell had depended on her daughter, and wasn't eager to see her go off to college. "Yes, but having a degree would make it so you could make more money. And what of your dream to be a nurse?"

"Maybe some dreams never come true."

Kira took the girl's hand and felt her tremble. "I know it seems hard right now, but you can do it. You are so talented."

She didn't look convinced.

"Okay, I won't push for now. Just don't blow off your finals."

"It's too late, I can't catch up."

"No, it's not too late. I've talked with both teachers. They'll give you makeup work, and if you do well on the final, you'll be okay. So you've got three days."

"But, I can't—"

"You can, because I'm going to help you," Kira insisted. "I want you back here after lunch."

Jody looked surprised. "Why? Why are you doing this?"

"Because I care about you, Jody. Right now you need to know that someone has faith in you. Someone cares."

Something Kira never had, until Trace. She just hadn't realized it soon enough. Now it was too late.

* * *

Trace paced the main room of the four room bunkhouse, but stopped to glance out the window. Kira was well-past due being home and there was a storm brewing. A big one. He checked his watch—it was after five o'clock.

"Why don't you just call her?" Cal said.

It was silly to act as if he didn't know who the foreman meant. "She's probably busy with graduation stuff. It's just she never pays attention to the weather."

"Then warn her." The wind picked up and lightning flashed in the dark sky.

Trace pulled out his phone and punched in Kira's number. When she didn't answer, he cursed his stubborn, independent wife and headed outside. The rain began falling in big drops and just as he reached his truck, her Jeep Cherokee pulled up next to the house. Anger mixed with relief as he ran toward her. Seeing her frightened look, he remained silent. He took her by the arm, rushed her up the steps and through the back door.

"Where the hell have you been?" he demanded as he forced the door shut against the strong wind.

Inside the mudroom, she put her briefcase down on the washing machine, then wiped the rain from her face. "I was helping a student, Jody Campbell, then I took her home."

"There's a severe storm warning. Didn't you hear it?"

"Not until I got into the car." She glanced out the window. "It's bad, isn't it?"

Another flash of lightning and the electricity went out. "I guess that answers your question."

He went to the pantry and pulled out the flashlight

and a box of candles. No matter how brave Kira acted, he knew she hated storms. He hurried back into the kitchen and shined the light toward her. "You okay?"

"Ask me after this storm passes."

"I don't think there's any chance of that for a while. There's a series of them across the area. It could go on all night." He called Cal on his cell. "How are things down there?"

"I'm heading over to the barn to check the horses. If there's any problems, I'll let you know."

He turned back to see Kira, lighting the half-used candles. The threatening clouds make it darker than normal at this time of day. They had a generator, but he didn't feel it was necessary right now.

The rain pelted against the roof, and Kira jumped at another flash of lightning, followed by the booming sound of thunder. "I should buy some new ones."

"Do you want to start up the generator?"

Kira sat down in the kitchen chair. "Not unless we have to go down to the basement."

Trace glanced out the window, but couldn't see anything with the blowing rain. "I'll check the forecast." He walked into the den they'd used as an office, and she followed. He had a battery-powered radio and flipped it on to the local weather channel.

"No tornados sighted in the area, so far. But the warnings won't be lifted for the area until after midnight."

She sighed. "I was afraid of that."

Even in the shadows, he could see her hand pressed against her stomach. Something he'd seen her doing many times during their marriage. It helped ease the cramps that came with her monthly period. It also gave them the sad news that once again they'd failed, failed to conceive a child.

He released a breath. There had been far too many of those times. And it had only gotten worse after the fertility treatments. In the end he could hardly bear to continue to try for a baby, or watch her heartbreak when the same result had been repeated with no pregnancy.

Trace swallowed his own pain. "Come on, I'll fix you a cup of tea." He waited for her to stand, then led her back into the kitchen. He turned on the gas stove, then went to the cupboard and took out a mug and tea bags.

Waiting for the water to heat, Trace leaned against the counter and studied Kira. She was dressed for summer, in her bright blue T-shirt and a long, flowered skirt, covered mostly by a bulky sweater.

It wouldn't be sexy to anyone else, but he knew what lay underneath. Long smooth legs, and a cute bottom and curves that drove a man wild.

She looked up at him, and her sweater opened. He didn't stop his open examination of her breasts. Her nipples quickly hardened under the thin material. He felt his own body respond and he looked up at her dark eyes. He didn't have to ask her if she wanted him, he could see it in her heated gaze. God, she was easy to read. It was one of the many things he loved about her. She didn't play games when it came to sex. If she wanted him, she let him know. And she was definitely letting him know now.

Suddenly the teapot whistled and he shook away any thoughts about carrying this any further. He removed the kettle, poured the water into the cup and placed it in front of her.

"You hungry?"

She shook her head. "My stomach is a little unsettled."

Seeing the stress in her face, he asked, "Cramps?"

She nodded as if embarrassed.

"You should be in bed."

The rain pelted against the windows. "I'm not going upstairs in this storm."

"Did you at least take your medication?" He knew she hated to resort to the painkillers, but sometimes she didn't have a choice.

She didn't respond.

"Where is it?"

"The bathroom, upstairs."

Trace grabbed the flashlight and headed out toward the stairs. He went into the room they'd shared for the past five years. He felt like the intruder now. Lightning suddenly illuminated the space, showing the neatly made bed. Kira never would go off and forget to make it. Something he knew she'd learned early on in foster care.

He liked it messy. He liked her messy after making love in the early mornings. When the sun wasn't up just yet, and all was fresh and new, the problems were pushed aside and they were lost only in each other. He shook away the thought as a crash of thunder rumbled through the house.

He went into the medicine cabinet and grabbed her pills, then went to the closet and took out a pair of sweatpants and a sweatshirt, along with a pair of tennis shoes. He hurried back downstairs and handed her the bundle. "I thought you might be more comfortable in these."

She looked surprised and pleased. "Thank you."

He went to the sink and got her a glass of water. On his return she was already removing her skirt. He went to the refrigerator, making himself busy, trying to think about food, and not his wife stripping off her clothes.

She stopped and took the medicine with a drink of water.

"Lie down and try to relax."

He walked back to the refrigerator and took out some bread, lettuce and sliced ham. Then he grabbed a plate from the cupboard and prepared the tray, wishing that a pill could make the problems between them disappear.

Ever since the moment he'd fallen in love with Kira, he'd known there was something she'd kept back. A tiny part of her that she'd never shared with him. He figured it had something to do with her parents' death and her years in foster care.

Her one living relative was a grandmother, Beth Hyatt, but as far as he knew, Kira hadn't been in touch with her since their marriage. Whenever he asked about her family, Kira clammed up, only saying her parents had died when she was young.

Sometimes her eyes showed such sadness and no matter how much he'd reassured her, he couldn't make it go away. Could a child do what he never could?

Trace walked to the sofa and found Kira lying on her side, her legs pulled up, indicating she was still in pain. He placed the tray on the coffee table and sat down at one end. Without a word, he placed Kira's head on his lap. He reached under her sweatshirt and touched her warm skin. He began a slow, circular motion over her back and down her spine. In the past, this helped relax her and ease her suffering.

Kira shifted a little and released a soft moan. He continued to stroke her skin, feeling his own need surfacing, but he didn't have to touch Kira to want her. He could stand across a room and she'd just have to glance at him and he wanted her. Hell, he'd been sleeping in the bunkhouse these past weeks and it hadn't changed anything.

She groaned again, then started to roll over.

"Stay still," he said.

"I can't. My stomach hurts." She managed to turn over on her back. Without hesitation, he placed his hand on her abdomen and continued the gentle motion.

"Is this helping any?"

"Oh, yeah," she murmured. "You can stop in about an hour."

It killed him to see her in pain. With the progressive disease, her periods seemed to have gotten more and more painful. And no one could do much to help her.

"I expected you to be asleep before this." He ached to stretch out beside her, to hold her close.

She smiled sleepily. "The pills are doing a good job. Just don't tell my students I'm a druggie."

"Your secret is safe with me."

For a few moments, it seemed like old times. But it wasn't and he had better remember that. Playful words didn't make a marriage work.

But he sure as hell would like to know what did.

* * *

Kira was in heaven. She didn't know if it was the pain medication or the fact that Trace was there holding her. She liked this dream. She fought the drugging sleep because she didn't want to wake up and find him gone again.

She felt him get up, then before she could protest, he lifted her into his arms. "Trace?" She couldn't even open her eyes.

"Shh, darlin', the worst of the storm is over and I'm taking you up to bed."

She smiled and curled in closer to his warmth. "Oh, I like the sound of that." But suddenly she felt the soft mattress as he laid her down and pulled away.

"Don't go," she whispered as she reached for him. "Please, Trace, don't leave me."

She felt his weight on the mattress, then his reassuring words. "I won't, Kira. I'm here."

With his comforting words, she let herself drift off to sleep. She felt his kiss against her hair. For the first time in weeks she allowed herself to think that maybe everything would be all right.

Kira's comfort was gone by morning when she woke up and found herself alone. There was no sign of Trace, or that he'd been there during the night. Even though she wanted to stay in bed, she got up, into the shower, then dressed for work.

Downstairs, she found coffee already made and poured herself a cup. She went to the window and glanced at the sunny morning and a deserted bunkhouse. Trace's truck was gone, too.

Disappointed, she knew he and Cal were probably

out checking the herd. She wondered if there was any damage to the outer buildings. Would Trace even tell her if there were? He'd always been pretty close-mouthed about the running of the ranch.

She'd shown more interest in the first couple of years after they were married. Once they'd started concentrating on a baby, she'd stopped horseback riding.

Looking back, she realized how much she'd pulled away from him with her self-absorbed guilt about not being able to conceive a baby. Trace had only been loving and supportive, never saying anything about the cost of medical procedures their insurance didn't pay for. That had been thousand of dollars.

That only added to her guilt. And when Trace suggested they take a break from trying, she blew up. Didn't talk to him for a week, then they fought some more, saying things that hurt. Things they couldn't take back. She drove him away, first emotionally, then finally, physically he packed his clothes up and moved to the bunkhouse.

Kira went to the sink and poured her coffee out. Not her proudest moment. She loved Trace more than anything, but she had to push and push to see if once again someone she loved left her. And he had.

Kira brushed a tear from her cheek.

Trace didn't have a clue about what was going on inside her. But it wasn't his fault. In the past, she'd only let him see what she wanted him to see.

She'd been unfair to him, but most importantly right now, she hadn't been honest, either. That had to change if they were going to survive. He deserved to know the truth. But, after all this time, could she take the chance that he might not forgive her?

Did it even matter? In six months, she'd lose Trace forever.

CHAPTER FOUR

By NOON the next day, the heat was pounding against Trace's back. It was nearly unbearable to work, but he kept going. They had to get the storm-damaged roof replaced on the feed barn.

"Man, you'd think the rain would cool things off," Cal said, as he took off his hat and wiped his forehead on his sleeve.

Trace moved another shingle into place, knowing he had no extra money to replace it. "We're in for more rain tonight. So we better get this done, or we'll lose all the hay and feed."

"It was one heck of a storm, but at least they got the electricity back on this morning." Cal reached for a nail and hammer. "I bet Kira was frightened. I wasn't surprised when you didn't come back to the bunkhouse last night."

Trace continued to work. "She wasn't feeling well. Once she took some medication, she finally fell asleep. I guess I did, too."

"Looks like I'll be losing a roommate soon."

"It doesn't look like that to me," Trace argued. "Nothing is settled."

Cal grinned. "If you say so."

"Damn, straight, I say so." Trace pounded in a nail for emphasis. "Can you get more work done and do less talking?"

"Sure, boss." Cal glanced toward the road. "But I doubt you will." He nodded to the black, luxury sedan. "Seems Jarrett has found you again."

Trace turned around to see his brother climb out of the car. This was not what he needed today. "I better go get this over with."

Trace made his way down the ladder and caught up with his brother at the corral gate. Jarrett was dressed in tailored navy slacks, a fitted white dress shirt and Italian loafers that probably cost more than Trace's entire wardrobe.

"Hey, I thought I told you to come by the office."

"I've been busy," Trace said. That was the only excuse he was giving him.

"We're all busy, but this is business. Didn't want to say anything the other day with Kira there but the loan payment is due."

"Not until the end of June," Trace corrected. "Don't worry you'll get your money." He started to walk away, but Jarrett stopped him.

"Hey, I'm not here to hound you. I'm here to make you an offer."

Trace frowned. His brother never did anything unless it benefited him. "Not interested."

"Come on, Trace. You haven't even given me a chance."

"Okay, what is it?"

"How about I buy back that southwest section of land? Then your loan will be paid in full."

Trace remained silent for a moment, knowing without a doubt his brother was up to something. "Are you going to develop that section?"

Jarrett shrugged. "Eventually, when the market recovers. Westchester Ridge is growing with new businesses and housing will be needed." He glanced toward the mountains. "There's a lot of pretty scenery around here."

"And I plan to keep it that way. We've talked about this, Jarrett, I'm not crazy about running cattle up to a tract of homes." He started to walk away.

"What if I put in writing that I won't develop that section of land for ten years? Would you be willing to listen then?"

"What is it with you? When Dad and Mom died you couldn't wait to unload your share of the ranch. I bought you out, now you want some back." He shook his head. "What are you up to?"

Jarrett's gaze darted away. "I'm not at liberty to talk about it now."

"Well, then I'm not talking, either."

"I guess I'll just wait until you lose it all," his brother called to him.

"I haven't lost anything. You'll get your money."

"Sure you can afford it?" He cocked an eyebrow. "Adoption can get pretty expensive."

Trace's chest tightened. Of course Jarrett would have been contacted by the agency. "I'm handling it. Now, I need to get back to work." He marched off, refusing to argue any longer with his brother.

Mostly Trace hated that he didn't have all the money. He was going to have to come up with some other way to pay off the loan. Worse, how was he going to be able to give Kira what she wanted, too?

After getting Mrs. Fletcher's phone call that morning, Kira finished her appointments at school and hurried home. The counselor had asked if she could move up the interview time for today instead of Monday. Kira would have liked the rest of the week to prepare, but she couldn't say no.

Except she couldn't get ahold of Trace. She'd been calling him for hours, but kept getting his voice mail. It was nearly one o'clock when Kira pulled into the driveway. She rushed into the house and put on a pot of coffee, then straightened up the kitchen. She called down to the bunkhouse and left a message for Trace. Then tried his cell phone again, before noticing it on the table. He must have left it last night.

A shiver went through her as she recalled the feel of his arms around her. The way she felt pressed against his strong body during the storm. Kira wanted that again. If only she could convince Trace to come back home, and back into their marriage.

Kira's thoughts turned to the possibility of a baby. Is that what Mrs. Fletcher would tell them today? There was also the intense scrutiny for an adoption. They could dig up a lot of things from her past. They knew about her time in foster care. All those years she hadn't shared with Trace.

He deserved to know the truth.

There was a knock on the back door. Kira took a calming breath, put on a smile and opened the door to find a middle-aged woman with a big smile and warm blue eyes.

"Kira McKane?" she began, "I'm Lucy Fletcher from Places in the Heart Agency."

"Welcome, Mrs. Fletcher. Please, come in."

Kira stepped back and allowed the woman to walk inside the big farm kitchen.

"Oh, this is lovely." She glanced around the newly remodeled room. There were maple cabinets and natural stone countertops and the walls were painted a spring green.

"Thank you. My husband and I remodeled right after we were married. I just wish I could spend more time at home." Kira directed her to the round table. And they sat down.

Mrs. Fletcher opened her briefcase and took out a file. "I know you've worked with Jessica Long for the past several months, but I'm taking over some of her cases while she's recovering from surgery. I hope that's not a problem."

"Not at all."

"Good. When opportunities arise, there's no time to wait." She glanced over the paper. "You're a high school guidance counselor. So are you planning to stay home if you have a child?"

Kira hesitated. She wanted to, if they could afford it.

"There's no wrong answer, Kira. It's hard these days to make it without two incomes."

"I'd like to stay home, of course, but adoption is expensive."

Mrs. Fletcher nodded. "It's true you have to help

absorb the expenses of the biological mother. One good thing about working in the school system, you have holidays and the summers off." She glanced around. "Is your husband going to be here today?"

"I hope so. I just realized that he left his cell phone here on the table this morning. And after the storm he needed to check for damage. He usually comes in for lunch."

"Good, I'm anxious to meet him." She smiled. "Why don't you show me your lovely home?"

"Sure." Kira took a breath and stood. "Would you like to see the nursery?"

"Eventually. Maybe we can start downstairs."

Kira relaxed some as they made their way through the rooms until the tour finally ended upstairs in the master bedroom. The walls were painted a soft blue, to offset the large, dark furniture.

She had made the bed this morning, but she couldn't help but recall last night with Trace. How he held her so tenderly. She quickly shook away the memory.

"The antique furniture belonged to my husband's grandparents. I discovered it in the attic after we were married. I don't think Trace was crazy about bringing it down."

"It's beautiful."

The next room across the hall was the nursery. Kira hesitated, then opened the door. It had been a while since she'd come in here. The walls were a buttery-yellow, with an old rocker she'd sanded and painted white. And there was a hand-carved cradle that had been in Trace's family for generations.

"Oh, this is lovely." Mrs. Fletcher walked to the row of windows that overlooked the pasture. "I see you are prepared." She went to the cradle. "Is this another treasure from the attic?"

Kira nodded. "I know we'll need a proper baby bed, but it's hard to get too excited, yet. I don't want to be disappointed."

"I hope that isn't the case, too." Mrs. Fletcher gave her a soft smile. "You and your husband have been very cooperative, releasing all your records to us." She glanced down at her notes. "We've just received your medical file states that you have advanced endometriosis. No miscarriages, but a live birth."

Kira hesitated, then knew she couldn't risk a lie and cause her to lose this chance. "Yes."

Mrs. Fetcher blinked in surprise. "You have a child?"

Kira's heart drummed against her chest, she paused, then rushed on to tell the social worker what she'd never told anyone. "Yes, I had a child fifteen years ago. I…I gave him up for adoption."

"I see." Lucy Fletcher studied her, then said, "I appreciate you telling me, Kira."

"Do you think this will hurt our chances for a baby?"

"Of course not." The woman touched her hand. "I believe you did what was best for everyone, especially the child."

Just then Kira glanced up and caught sight of her freshly showered husband standing in the doorway. Panic froze her, seeing the intense look from him.

Mrs. Fletcher turned around. "Oh, you must be Trace. I'll Lucy Fletcher from Places in the Heart. I've looked forward to meeting you."

Trace accepted her hand and shook it. "It's nice to

meet you, too. Sorry, I'm late, I needed to shower off the mud."

"We did get quite the storm last night, didn't we."

"And I needed to do some repairs first thing this morning."

Kira couldn't help but wonder how much of the conversation Trace had overheard. "I explained to Mrs. Fletcher you forgot to take your cell phone with you. So I couldn't get hold of you."

Mrs. Fletcher stepped in. "I've enjoyed spending time talking with your wife while she showed me around your beautiful home."

"Kira has done most of the decorating." Trace stood beside her, but he didn't touch her.

"Well, if you have a few minutes, Trace, I'd like to talk with you both."

"Let's go downstairs," Kira suggested, praying there wouldn't be any more talk about her past. She led them into the dining room, then went to get the coffee.

In the kitchen, Kira willed herself to stop shaking. If Trace overheard she'd deal with it. If he hadn't she needed to tell him. Everything. With a calming breath, she returned to the dining room table with coffee and cookies. She sat down next to Trace. He continued to answer questions she knew he'd been asked before by the other counselor.

Finally Lucy Fletcher sat back and eyed the two of them. "Would you both be available again on Monday afternoon?"

Kira immediately nodded. "Of course."

Trace hesitated. "You have more questions?"

Mrs. Fletcher shook her head. "I'm in agreement

with Jessie Long that you two would make wonderful parents. It's a birthmother who wants to speak with you."

"Birthmother?" Kira said, barely capable of breathing.

"Yes. I gave her your file and she's asked for a home visit." Mrs. Fletcher smiled. "She has chosen you two as possible parents for her baby."

Heart pounding, Kira glanced at Trace, unable to read his thoughts. She turned back to Mrs. Fletcher. "She wants to meet us?"

"You said you don't have a problem with an open adoption. Have you changed your mind?"

"No! It's just I didn't expect it would happen so fast."

"Sometimes that's how it works. So is Monday afternoon okay?"

Kira didn't know how to answer, but Trace took it out of her hands. "Monday will be fine."

Mrs. Fletcher stood. "Good. We'll see you here then."

Kira walked the woman out and stood on the porch until she got in her car and drove off. Hugging herself, she tried to control her trembling as a hundred thoughts raced through her head. A baby. Were they really going to get a baby?

Her excitement died knowing she had to face Trace. Had he heard their conversation? And how was she going to try to explain why she'd kept her past a secret? What if Mrs. Fletcher brought it up again? She turned to go back into the house, praying Trace still cared for her enough to listen to her reasons.

Inside, she found Trace carrying the cups to the

sink. He didn't look at her. Instead he busied himself with the cleanup.

She couldn't let him shut her out again. "Do you have time to talk before you go back to work?"

He grabbed the towel and wiped his hands off, then looked at her. "Don't you think it's a little late for that now?"

Trace had gotten Kira's voice message on the bunk-house phone. Filthy, he'd jumped into the shower and dressed before he'd headed to the house to meet with Mrs. Fletcher. He'd known how important this was to Kira, and to him, too. He was willing to go through another round of invasive questions. Anything to help Kira. So she could have the child she'd always dreamed of.

He heard Kira's voice from the nursery, but by the time he went into the room, she'd stopped talking. She'd looked surprised to see him there. But wasn't he supposed to play a part in this?

"What do you mean there's nothing to talk about?" Kira asked.

"It seems already settled and Monday we're going to be talking to a woman about raising her child. It's what you want, Kira."

She looked hurt. "You agreed for her to come here. Please tell me now if you've changed your mind."

Trace's mind was reeling. He didn't realize it would be this hard. He'd be lying if he said he didn't want a child with Kira, but like this? He began to think about the next six months, living in the same house. Just walking by her and inhaling her heavenly scent. He would never feel her warmth, her softness against him. When he raised his head, those big brown eyes stared up at him, mesmerizing him.

All the things he would lose forever. This short time was all they had together. Was this the only way he could be a part of her life?

"It's happening so fast," he said.

"Isn't it better this way?" she asked.

Trace studied Kira. He could see the strain on her face, knew how anxious she was. She wanted a baby, even at the cost of their marriage.

He walked toward her. "This is life changing, Kira. You're taking on a lot by yourself, trying to raise a baby."

"I don't have a choice."

"There's always a choice." He stared down at her. He wanted her. If only to taste her mouth, bury himself into her body. But that would be a temporary fix for their problems.

He sighed. He had some thinking to do.

"I've got to get back to work." He practically ran out, more frightened than he'd ever been in his life that he could lose everything. And he wasn't talking about the ranch.

Later that afternoon, Kira stood in the Winchester Ridge High School auditorium, trying to concentrate on the graduation rehearsal that was going on. But it wasn't working. Between her lack of sleep, and the earlier visit from Mrs. Fletcher, her head was all over the place.

Especially Trace's disappearance. She'd planned to

try to talk to him some more, but he conveniently couldn't be found. Worse, her plan had backfired. She'd hoped for some enthusiasm about the possibility of getting a baby, instead Trace was off brooding.

The last thing she wanted was to end their marriage. She loved Trace. When the letter arrived from the agency, she'd hoped her husband wanted to work on saving it, too.

Now with the graduation ceremony tomorrow, she had no choice but to be at school. Then she had to get through the class roundup Saturday before the seniors would go off for the summer. After that she would have Trace alone. They couldn't go on avoiding each other. She knew she'd pushed him away over the past year with her mood swings, her needy attitude. That wasn't going to happen again.

She sighed. In the beginning of their marriage it was simple. He'd loved her, and she'd loved him. Then with her difficulties to conceive a baby, things had turned sour. Instead of turning to each other, they'd turned away. So how could she ask him to just forget everything and convince him to be her husband again? So instead she offered him a divorce with no strings. She just prayed he wouldn't take it.

Tears burned behind her eyes. What she wanted more than anything else was the chance to make another go of their marriage. Maybe if she'd been honest with him from the start things would be different, but she couldn't even tell him about the child she'd given away. The child who claimed a big piece of her heart.

Hearing her name called brought her back to the

present. Kira looked up in time to see the last of the students march across the stage as the principal handed them a substitute diploma. Then they all returned to their seats, the recessional march played and the students filed out. Kira followed them. Once outside she gathered the group for last minute instructions.

"Another thing, class," she began, then looked up feeling her throat tighten. She'd known most of these kids since they were freshmen. Now, some were going off to college, some to the military and others into the work force. She only prayed that she'd given them enough help to survive. More than she ever got at their age.

"This is the last time I'm going to be able to say that." She looked up at Jason Rush, Steve Matthews and Michael Begay. All of them were well over six feet tall. "It's been a delight to have you all this past year," she said, fighting the emotions. "I'd like to continue our friendships, so please…please, when you celebrate be smart. Please don't drink and drive."

She reached up and tapped Steve on the side of the head playfully. "I worked too hard for any of you to end up as roadkill on the highway."

The group released a groan.

"No, I don't want to hear any excuses. I just want your promise."

There were disgruntled murmurs of response, then the group dispersed. All except Jody Campbell. She seemed to be hanging back. Maybe she wanted to talk again. Kira walked toward the young woman.

"Do you need a ride home, Jody?"

"I can walk," the girl said as she hugged her slim body. She looked too thin in her baggy jeans and T-shirt.

Kira glanced up at the threatening clouds as the wind began to pick up. "Come on, Jody. If I don't give you a ride you'll get drenched."

The girl reluctantly followed Kira to the car. Once they were inside the Jeep Cherokee, the sky opened up. Hearing the rain pelt the top of the car, Kira decided to wait out the downpour. She looked across the seat at her sullen passenger.

"You know, Jody, I'm proud of you. You managed to ace your finals and save some of your grade-point average."

"I lost out on first honors, though." She shrugged. "Oh, well, I'm not going to college anyway."

Kira hated it when any of her students gave up. "Jody, there are other ways to go to school than going away. You can attend community college."

Jody brushed her blond hair from her shoulders and stared out the rain streaked window. "I told you my mom can't afford for me to go to college."

"You could apply for a student loan," Kira suggested. "I'll help you fill out the paperwork."

Jody turned to her. Tears clouded her eyes. "I don't want your help." She began to sob. "You're wasting your time on me."

"Don't say that, Jody, you're worth every bit of my time."

The girl glanced away. "It doesn't matter anymore, nothing matters." She started to climb out, but Kira reached for her.

"It matters, Jody. Please, don't be so hard on yourself. I promise I won't talk about college. Just tell me you're coming to the roundup."

"I have to work that day."

"That's a shame since you've worked so hard on organizing the party. You've got to come, Jody."

The girl hesitated.

"I promise it'll be the last thing I'll ever ask of you. Come on, you need to celebrate."

"I'll try," the girl said, then jumped out of the car, and ran off in the rain.

Kira didn't go after her. She knew from her own experience that she couldn't make Jody confide in her if she didn't want to. But Kira was going to be darn sure that she was there for her. And she had a strange feeling the girl was going to need her.

Trace was angry with himself for riding Thunder so hard. And what had it accomplished? Nothing. He climbed down and immediately removed the saddle and blanket, then began walking the lathered horse around to cool him down.

"Sorry, fella. You're the one who had to put up with my bad mood today."

Twenty minutes later, Trace led him into the barn and stall, then started brushing him.

"Did the ride help your mood?"

Trace looked over the stall gate to see Cal.

"Probably not." He stopped brushing. "I've got a lot on my mind. You have a problem with that?"

He shook his head. "You're the boss. I'll just stay out of your way." Cal started to leave, then stopped. "Is the senior roundup still on? Are the kids still coming?"

"As far as I know it is, but maybe you should ask Kira."

Cal looked past him toward the doorway and smiled. "I think I will. Hi, Kira, we were just talking about you."

Trace glanced over his shoulder and saw her. She was dressed in jeans and a red and blue print blouse. Her hair was pulled back, showing off the delicate line of her jaw, the softness of her skin.

"Hi, Jonas." She nodded. "Trace."

He didn't have much to say back. "Cal wants to know about the roundup."

"That's why I'm here." She directed her attention to Trace. "I need to double-check on things."

"As long as I have bodies to bring in the herd, you can do whatever you want." The last thing Trace wanted to do was pretend that everything was perfect between them all day, but why disappoint the kids.

"You sure?" she asked. "With the day of activities, the music and dancing afterward? It's a long day."

"Why would it be any different than in the past four years?" Senior roundup had been Trace's idea after they'd first gotten married.

"Because it is different this year," she told him.

"I've got things to take care of," Cal said and disappeared from the barn.

"That's separate," he said, continuing to brush Thunder. "The roundup has nothing to do with us."

"Trace, it all has everything to do with us." She came to the railing. "I guess we can put off the personal stuff until the roundup is over. But we can't ignore the fact that there is a counselor and birthmother coming Monday."

He closed his eyes a second and took a breath.

"Surely we can get through a day together. Call it practice for our interview to see if we qualify as the perfect parents."

When he opened the gate and stepped out, she touched his arm to stop him. "I know the past few months have been hard, but is it that difficult to act as if you care about me? My feelings for you haven't changed, Trace, I love you." She rose up on her toes. Her hand slid up his chest, burning a path of need that threatened to destroy his resolve.

With a groan, Trace captured her mouth in an eager kiss, hating his weakness for her. Yet, it didn't stop his wanting her, needing her. He drew her against his body, hoping to ease some of the ache. It didn't. He released her with a jerk, his breathing labored. Seeing the desire in her rich brown eyes, he had to glance away.

"You can't deny you still care about me," she argued.

"A few heated kisses doesn't make a marriage, Kira." His gaze moved over her pretty face, unable to ignore the hurt his words caused her. He cupped her face. "I couldn't give you what you wanted then, Kira. I'm not sure I can now."

So why in the hell did he want to try so badly?

CHAPTER FIVE

I COULDN'T give you what you wanted, and I'm not sure I can now.

Trace's words still echoed in her head as Kira walked out to the back porch at dawn on Saturday. Over the last forty-eight hours she tried to stay hopeful. Hopeful that he would say yes to staying with her during the adoption process. It was a perfect opportunity to work on their marriage. That was if he still wanted to be a part of her life, and their baby's life.

All those answers had to be put off until the roundup was over. Once alone Sunday night, they could discuss things and make a decision before the biological mother's visit on Monday.

Trace had stayed away from the house as he prepared for the roundup. And even though she'd had the graduation to help supervise, Kira still found time to think about the future.

Would it include Trace, and a baby?

Now she just had to get through this day, the senior roundup. Kira stepped off the back porch and walked toward the rows of tables that had been set up the night before by the graduates' parents, grateful their kids would have a safe place to celebrate. To protect the guests and the food from the hot sun, several canopies shaded the area. A big banner hung across the barn that read, Winchester Ridge High School Senior Roundup, Class Of 2009.

Kira smiled. She loved doing the party. Both Trace and she had enjoyed it the past. And as far as she could tell, he was okay with it this year, too.

Some of the senior boys had showed up ready to ride in the roundup. They were gathering in the corral with their mounts. Then she saw Trace lead Thunder out of the barn and head to the group. She watched him give directions to the men, then grabbed hold of the saddle horn and easily swung onto his mount.

Panic rose in Kira when she realized that he was ready to leave without saying goodbye. Then he looked in her direction, giving her a sliver of hope that he wanted her to send him off like she had in the past. Trace shouted something to Cal, then walked his horse in the opposite direction, toward her.

Kira caught up to him about halfway. "You're leaving already?"

He nodded and watched the group of men walking their horses through the gate toward the range. "I want to have the herd back by ten. Barring any problems, we should be."

Nodding, she stepped closer to stroke Thunder, but the animal was anxious to take off, too. "The rest of the kids should be here by then to help with the branding."

He tugged on the reins to get the stallion back under control. "I'll send one of the hands back ahead of us."

He hesitated. "Just to make sure none of the kids get in the way. I don't want anyone to get hurt."

"We have some of the dads assigned to help out."

She couldn't take her eyes off Trace, and the way he handled the horse. In jeans and a chambray shirt, he wore his usual belt with the large buckle with the McK brand. It had belonged to his grandfather.

"Be careful," she said, placing her hand on his knee. If the contact bothered him, he didn't let on. Darn. "And tell the men there'll be plenty of good food waiting for them."

He cocked an eyebrow. "Will there be some of your potato salad?"

The request surprised her. "I might be persuaded to whip up a batch." She already had it made and chilling in the refrigerator.

She'd been encouraged after he'd kissed her last night, knowing he was fighting his feelings toward her. She wasn't going to make it easy for him, either. She stared at him, catching his incredible gray eyes.

"Be careful today."

"I'm not foolish, especially with green kids to look out for."

Her fingers flexed against his knee. "Just make sure you look out for you, too."

Trace started to speak, but someone whistled to him. He glanced at the riders off in the distance. "I've got to go."

"Stay safe." She stepped back as he tugged his hat lower, kicked Thunder's sides and they shot off. She trembled as she watched until he disappeared over the horizon.

"Now, I'd say that man wants to stay married."

Kira gasped as she swung around. She found her friend smiling at her. "Michele. I didn't expect you so soon."

Her fellow counselor smiled. "You weren't exactly paying attention. So I take it things are okay with you two?"

Kira released a breath. "It isn't that simple." She knew she had to tell Trace everything. "There's a lot we need to deal with."

Her friend frowned. "Maybe you should skip the talking and go straight to…other things."

That had never been the problem. "I can't rush Trace." Kira had never lived in one place long enough to make any close friends. Not before Michele.

"Well, if it were me, I'd hang onto that cowboy any way I could." Michele looked around. "Um, do you think Jarrett is going to show up today?"

Kira frowned, surprised at her friend's question. "Why would Jarrett come today? He's never helped out before, well, not since I've been here."

"I ran into him at the diner yesterday." Michele shrugged. "I told him about today, and he said he might drop by."

Kira studied her. Michele was interested in her brother-in-law? "Well, if he does it's because he wants something."

Michele grinned. "Yeah, and I'm hoping it's me. You're not the only one who wants a good-looking McKane man."

Three hours later, Trace was riding drag behind the herd. Thanks to the recent rain, there wasn't much dust kicked up. Just the steady sound of mamas calling to their calves.

He relaxed in the saddle, letting Thunder do the work as he glanced at the incredible scenery. North was the Roan Plateau and thick rows of tall pines of the White River National Forest. He had grown up in this area, hunted and fished here all his life. He never wanted to live anywhere else. He wanted to continue on the family tradition, to raise a family here on McKane land and hand it down to his kids.

Sadness took him by surprise. Now his marriage was possibly coming to an end. What was he supposed to do, just walk away and find someone else? Trouble was, there wasn't anyone else for him. He'd known that the second he'd laid eyes on Kira Hyatt. He fell in love. Now, she wanted to end it all.

Suddenly a few calves ran by and caught up with their mamas, then Cal rode up beside him.

"Did you get them all?"

The foreman nodded. "Yeah. Jerry's hanging back to make sure."

Trace glanced over nearly three hundred heads. "That's about a hundred and fifty calves to brand. It looks like we'll be busy today. If we get them separated fast, break for lunch, then we can work four teams on the branding irons and castrating. We should finish up by afternoon."

Cal grinned. "That's if those senior boys are willing to work. Remember there will be teenage girls hanging on the fence watching them."

"Then you'll have to keep them in line."

Trace could still remember Kira's first roundup, and

how distracted she'd made him. It was long before there had been a senior roundup. They had only been dating a few weeks. He shifted in the saddle, recalling that had been the first night he'd made love to her. He released a long breath. That seemed like another lifetime ago.

"Sure, boss," Cal said. "Are there any other miracles you want today?"

Trace remained quiet, but there was one. All he'd ever wanted was Kira, but it might take a miracle to save their marriage.

"They're coming," one of the kids yelled.

Kira climbed up on the stock pen fence, and excitement raced through her as she looked for Trace. It was hard not to be swept up in it. She could imagine a hundred years ago the ranchers' wives doing the same thing, cheering for their men as they brought in the herd.

About a dozen teenage girls were all decked out in their best Western clothes. Kira smiled. Some things never change. It was all about the boy getting the girl. She glanced down at her own dark denim jeans, and new teal Western-style blouse. Since she wasn't planning to do any branding, she could dress up, too.

Would Trace care, or would he be too busy with his work? In the past, he'd always noticed her. Maybe he didn't say a lot, but he couldn't hide his reaction.

When Cal rode in, he assigned jobs to the boys who were to help separate the calves from the cows. Mooing sounds filled the air as the first of the herd arrived. Things got busy as riders did their jobs to corral the herd.

Trace arrived and was busy shouting orders when suddenly a calf bolted away. He shot off after the wayward bovine. Kira was mesmerized watching the two, man and horse working in unison, cutting off the animal and forcing him back.

"Well, that was impressive," Michele said.

"Thunder is a great cutting horse."

"The cowboy isn't bad, either."

Kira finally smiled. "No, he's not." She glanced past her friend to see Jody arrive.

She started toward the girl who was dressed in faded jeans and a white blouse. She didn't have any fancy boots, just athletic shoes. The girl reminded Kira so much of herself at that age.

"Jody, I'm so glad you could make it."

"I can't stay too late. My mom can't pick me up."

"Then I'll take you home," Kira offered. "You're not missing all the fun."

"But I didn't bring anything to wear to the dance tonight."

Kira smiled. "I have something you can wear," she whispered. "I'm sure we can find something you like."

Jody looked surprised. "Really?"

Kira nodded as another classmate, Laura Carson, came up to them. "Please stay, Jody. This is our last time the class will be together."

Jody glanced around, sadness etched on her face. "But Ben's here."

"So what?" Laura said. "He's a jerk anyway. We'll hang out together."

"How about I put you two in charge of the food tables?"

The two friends exchanged smiles. "Okay."

"Then let's get the other girls together and haul the food out. The guys will finish soon and be hungry."

Jody and Laura gathered up some classmates and they headed off to the kitchen.

"Oh, to be that young and carefree again," Michele said.

Kira nodded, but realized she hadn't felt carefree since the day her parents died and she was left alone.

Trace had been busy most of the day, and so had Kira. Their paths had only crossed once when he'd gotten in line for the noon meal. She served him a plate of fried chicken, a big helping of potato salad and a smile.

He liked the smile the best.

Now, one hundred and forty-one calves had been branded, and eighty-seven castrated into steers which he'd once planned to run in a summer herd. But with the loan payment coming due, he needed to sell them off now, along with some of his heifers. If he got enough money, he could hang on to his breeding bulls a while longer. They were a big part of their future and keeping the ranch going.

A dark sedan car pulled into the driveway, catching Trace's attention. The tall, athletic, Jarrett McKane climbed out and walked toward him with that cocky attitude that demanded people's attention. And he got it.

Trace was surprised, but more suspicious of his brother's casual appearance in faded jeans and a dark Western shirt. What reason would Jarrett have to show up at the roundup?

Trace's thoughts turned to his older brother's business

proposition. It would be easy to hand back the land, but he knew Jarrett had never felt the same way he did about the ranch. If someone wanted it, for the right price, his brother would sell. Somebody had to want that section of land—and badly—for Jarrett to work so hard to get it back.

"Hey, bro, I hear you could use some help," Jarrett said.

"I'd say you were a little late. We finished the branding a while ago. But if you really want to help out, Cal can use your help separating the yearlings." He raised an eyebrow. "That is, if you still remember how to ride a horse."

His brother's eyes narrowed. "As I recall, I've beaten you in a few rodeos."

Jarrett had beaten him in a lot of things. "Then prove it."

"I will, but first, I need to say hello to a few people."

Trace took hold of his arm. "I won't have you wheeling and dealing at Kira's school function."

"You're pretty protective of the little mother-to-be."

Trace stiffened as he glanced around. "I'd appreciate it if you'd keep that to yourself. Nothing is definite yet."

Jarrett relented. "Sure."

"I mean it, Jarrett."

"Okay. Okay." He pulled away and walked off, but slowed his gait when Michele Turner came toward him. Then together the two went toward the branding pens.

"Trace."

He turned around to see Kira. He put on a smile. "How's it going?"

"Good, so far. We're just about to start the contests.

Are you able to help with the cutting competition? Mark Petersen is going to handle steer wrestling, and Cal will do the roping."

Trace shook his head. "Where do these kids get so much energy?" They started walking toward the branding pen. "I could use a nap."

She smiled. "I wouldn't mind one, either."

His gaze locked with hers. "You think they'd notice if we disappeared?"

Kira swallowed hard, and turned away. "Yeah, I think so."

Trace's body tensed. He tried not to remember those past lazy afternoons when they'd go up to the bedroom and make love for hours. Where had those carefree days gone?

"I better get going," he murmured, then turned and walked away. He quickened his steps. He didn't need to be thinking about Kira right now, especially since they hadn't been intimate in months.

He groaned and kept walking. Today was about the kids. He needed to keep his desire for Kira out of it.

A nearly impossible task.

Kira stood at the corral fence along with the other kids and parents, watching Trace work Thunder. She'd always been in awe of her husband's skill with horses. He looked so at ease on the powerful stallion, but there was no doubt who was in charge. Trace.

She glanced down at his gloved hands. She knew that along with that power came gentleness. A shiver raced through her, recalling the nights he'd stroked her, caressed her body, bringing her endless pleasure.

"He's pretty good."

Kira fought a blush as she turned to find Jarrett next to her at the railing. "Yes, he is."

A mischievous grin appeared on his face. "That's because I taught him everything he knows."

Cheers broke out from the crowd. "Really?" She hadn't known her brother-in-law as a young man. And just barely got to know him better over the past few years because Trace and he weren't close. A few holidays here and there when their folks were alive. "Since I've never seen you on a horse, I can't judge."

"And you're loyal to your husband."

"Always."

"Lucky guy."

She'd known Jarrett was attracted to her when she first came to town. But the minute she saw Trace, she couldn't think of anyone else. "Okay, what do you want, Jarrett?"

"Can't I give my sister-in-law a compliment?" He looked toward the corral. "I know things have been rough for you both lately." He glanced around, then lowered his voice. "Well, what I mean is the adoption."

Of course Trace's brother would be interviewed by the agency. She stepped down from the railing and Jarrett followed her away from the other people. "We're still in the beginning stages. I'd appreciate it if you kept it quiet for now."

"Of course." He paused. "I never realized that things... I mean I know you two wanted kids, but I never dreamed it was like this."

She managed a smile and touched his arm. "It's okay, Jarrett. I've accepted it," she lied, not wanting to go over this now, or with him.

He nodded. "Well, if there's anything I can do. There's a doctor I knew in college. He's made a name for himself in the fertility field."

It was nice that he wanted to help, but they'd already been to two specialists. "Thank you, Jarrett. We've been to doctors, and it hasn't helped." She blinked back tears. "Hopefully adoption will give us the family we want." She told him about the appointment on Monday.

"That's great news." He hugged her. "Is there anything I can do to help? I know it's expensive."

Kira started to answer, when she heard, "We can handle it."

They both turned to see Trace.

She stepped back from Jarrett, seeing the look on her husband's face. Jealousy? "Trace. I thought you were working with the kids."

He moved up beside her and stood close. "Cal and some of the other hands are handling the competition." He looked at her, but his gray eyes were unreadable. "Thought you might need some help."

She managed to pull her gaze away from his. "I've just been waiting for the DJ to set up for the dance. Jody Campbell organized everything, she's assigned all the kids with a job." She glanced around the area. "Maybe I should go find her. If you men will excuse me."

Trace watched Kira walk off. He wanted to go after her, and he would, just as soon as he figured out why his brother was here.

"Okay, what's going on, Jarrett?"

"I told you, I just came by to help out. You should have called me about the roundup."

"I've called you for help over the years. You've

always been busy. Why is the ranch suddenly important to you?"

"Just because I don't want to run the place doesn't mean I don't care about the ranch."

"Then prove it. Don't call in my loan in thirty days. Give me more time."

Jarrett hesitated. "If you really don't have the money, do you think you can keep the ranch going?"

"Yes, the ranch is making money. I just have other expenses." He hated telling his brother the details. "Like you said, adopting a baby is expensive. If I need to, I'll sell off my breeding bulls."

Jarrett looked distracted, and Trace caught Michele walking toward them. "Come by my office next week, we'll talk." Jarrett rushed off before Trace could say anything.

Trace had wanted to look up to his older brother, but years of watching him take from people and receive all the benefits of the favored son had changed that.

The one time Trace came in first had been with Kira, when she'd chosen him over his brother. Now, he could lose her, too. If that happened, it didn't matter if he kept the ranch, or not.

CHAPTER SIX

THE afternoon was in full swing as Trace kept busy sharing his expertise with the kids. He had Jake Petersen on Thunder, instructing him on the art of cutting.

Kira noticed that the teenage girls were watching intently. Most of the females were eyeing the boys, but a few of the mothers had their attention square on her husband.

Had Trace noticed it, too? Did he notice the other women? Desire other women? A woman who could give him a child?

Suddenly cheers broke out in the arena as Jake completed his task. The boy pumped his fist in the air in celebration. Kira smiled, refusing to let anything interfere with this great day. It was for the kids. Next, Ben Kerrigan climbed on the horse and began his turn. Although he wasn't as successful, the crowd cheered him on. All except for Jody.

Kira noticed the teenage girl stayed back from the group, but when Ben got down from his ride, she was waiting for him at the corral gate. After talking a moment, Ben shook his head and stormed off.

Not good. Kira threw up a prayer, hoping it was nothing more serious than a silly fight, that she'd been wrong about a possible pregnancy. Something she knew about firsthand and could change your life, forever.

Kira heard her name called and turned around and saw Trace walking in her direction. "Want to try a turn at cutting?"

"You're kidding. You want me to make a fool of myself in front of the kids?"

"You're a good rider, Kira. I doubt you could ever look foolish." He tugged on her arm. "Come on, I dare you."

Just then a chant started amongst the kids. "Mrs. McKane. Mrs. McKane." That and Trace's sexy grin, she couldn't resist. The kids began to cheer as Trace led her to the horse. "Just remember it's been a long time since I've been on a horse."

"It's okay, Kira. I'll be close by," he assured her.

"Promise?" That had been something they used to say to each other.

He nodded. "Promise."

Kira tore her gaze away to concentrate on her task. She placed her foot in the stirrup and found Trace's hands on her waist, boosting her up. Once in the saddle, she pulled her cowboy hat down on her head to shield her eyes from the bright sunlight, then looked at her husband. "Refresh me on what to do."

"First of all, relax." He reached up and placed her hands on the horn, letting the reins go slack. "Let Thunder do the work."

"Yes, sir."

With a wink, he strolled to the side of the corral and

called out instructions. When one of the boys released a young steer, the cutting horse took off, twisting and turning, trying to maneuver the cow back toward the fence. Kira kept her legs pressed firmly against the horse and her hands on the saddle horn. It took a while but she relaxed as Thunder did his job, then the bell rang to signal time was up.

The kids broke into cheers as Trace came out to help her off. "You were great," he said, then surprised her with a quick kiss on the lips. The crowd roared with approval. A sudden heat rose to her face as Kira made her way back to the fence. *Don't make anything out of his attention,* she told herself. *It's only for show.*

Two classmates, Amy and Marcy, rushed to her. "Oh, Mrs. McKane, that was so cool," Amy gushed. "And Mr. McKane is so good-looking." Then the girls ran off giggling, quickly distracted by another boy riding Thunder.

Back to work. Kira turned her attention to the barn and the truck unloading the audio equipment for the dance in a few hours. At the patio area she saw the volunteer fathers starting up the barbecues for the hamburgers. She checked her watch to see that everything was on schedule.

"Mrs. McKane."

Kira turned around to see Jody and Laura hurrying toward her.

"Jody, Laura, are you having fun?"

They answered with smiles. "Oh, yes," Laura said. "We're going to eat soon. By then the DJ will be ready to start the music. Some of the girls want to change their clothes. I've put the Girls Only sign on the bunkhouse door."

Kira thought about the room that Trace had been staying in and wondered if he'd locked it. "Do you know what rooms to use?"

"Mr. McKane gave us permission to use three rooms and a bathroom. He said he locked the rooms we can't use. And Cal will make sure the boys stay away."

"Good. Laura, would you ask your mother to help supervise?"

"Sure. Come on, Jody."

Kira placed a hand on Jody. "I need her to help me with something first." Kira wanted Jody to stay for the evening, and if that meant finding her something to wear, then that's what she'd do. "She'll meet up with you later."

At the girl's nod, Kira took Jody to the house.

"You don't have to do this, Mrs. McKane."

"I know. But I want you to stay and enjoy the party. You're a graduate, this is supposed to be a wonderful time for you. Enjoy it."

They passed several mothers in the kitchen, setting out the leftovers for supper. With a promise to be back soon to help out, she took Jody through the house and up the stairs.

"Your house is so beautiful, Mrs. McKane."

"Thank you. It's my husband's family home." The first home she'd had in a very long time, since her parents' death. She wondered how much longer she would call it home.

Kira walked down the hall into the master bedroom, but when she turned around she'd lost her companion. Then she saw Jody across the hall in the nursery.

"Jody."

The girl jumped. "I'm sorry." She pointed to the cradle. "Are you going to have a baby?"

"Sadly, no." Kira forced a smile. "Trace and I would love to have a child, but so far, it hasn't happened."

"Oh. Sorry, I didn't mean to be nosy."

"It's okay." Kira nodded and together they walked into the master bedroom. She went to the closet and began the search. She pulled out a couple of gauzy skirts and a peasant blouse. Kira glanced at Jody. "What size are you, about a four?"

The girl hesitated, then nodded.

Kira stopped. "Don't worry, Jody. I've never worn these clothes to school. No one will know that they aren't yours. Besides, don't girls borrow clothes from friends?"

She nodded. "But you're my guidance counselor."

Kira smiled. "Not anymore."

Jody finally smiled, too. "I guess not."

"Okay, I think this multicolored skirt will work. It has kind of a Western look." She went to the dresser and took out a bright-pink, cotton top and a wide belt. Then she went to the closet again and found a denim jacket. "It'll get cool tonight." She glanced at the girl's white canvas shoes. "I think your shoes will work with the outfit, but if not, I have boots."

The teenager eyed the clothes draped on the bed. "These are so beautiful. What if something happens to them?"

"They're only clothes, Jody." Kira headed out. "When you leave, go out the front door and no one will see you. Now, you better get dressed. I'm depending on you to help supervise the party."

"Thank you, Mrs. McKane."

"You're welcome." Kira shut the door and was surprised to see Trace waiting for her in the hall. "Trace. Is there a problem?"

"No, but since the girls have taken over the bunkhouse, I was going to shower and change here. Then I heard you in there with Jody."

He was coming to their bedroom to change. "Can you wait a few minutes?"

"I could shower in the guest bath, but my good jeans and boots are in the closet," he suggested.

"You go and I'll bring you your clothes." She nudged him toward the bathroom.

He hesitated. "Have I told you what a great job you're doing today?" He jerked a nod toward their bedroom. "And getting Jody something to wear was awfully nice of you."

She shrugged. "She doesn't have the money to dress like the other kids." Kira glanced away. "I know what it's like to be different. To feel left out."

He only nodded, then went to the bath, and closed the door. Soon, she heard the sound of the water running in the shower.

The bedroom door opened and Jody stepped out. "Oh, Jody, you look so cute," Kira told her.

"You think so?"

"Yes, just let me put a little makeup on you," She guided her into the bathroom. Ten minutes later, she'd fixed her hair and added color to the girl's cheeks. Pleased with her work, Kira sent Jody off to her friends.

Trace felt foolish sneaking down the hall in his own house, practically naked. And he wasn't about to put on his dirty clothes. Not hearing a sound, he peered into the bedroom. His heart shot off pounding when he found Kira standing in front of the full-length mirror. She had on a bright pink and green sundress, and a matching sweater. Her hair was pulled back from her pretty face, hoop earrings hung from each delicate lobe.

She turned and suddenly gasped when she saw him. "Trace. Oh, I'm sorry, I forgot your clothes."

"It's okay. Is the coast clear?" He glanced around, then stepped inside, closing the door behind him.

He couldn't help but notice how her gaze roamed over him. It was so intense it felt like a caress. His breath grew labored, his body definitely aware. "I need to shave. Are you finished in the bath."

"Oh, yes, of course."

In the past, he'd play this little game and they'd end up in bed. Now, they both seemed awkward, unable to speak. He walked across the room into the bathroom they'd once shared. It smelled of Kira, her shampoo, her body spray.

He drew a breath like a suffocated man.

She came to the doorway. "I should get back to the party."

He opened the cabinet and was surprised to find all his things still there. He took out his shaving cream. "It should only take me ten minutes and I'll be down." He found he liked her standing there, watching. It was like so many times they'd shared and taken for granted. He caught her reflection in the mirror as he applied the cream to his jaw. She still hadn't left.

"You did a nice thing for Jody."

She shrugged. "It's important she feel good about herself."

He took a swipe across his jaw with the razor. "I'd say you helped her with that tonight."

"Kids can be cruel."

Trace knew that Kira was talking about herself. Although she never talked much about her life in foster care, he knew it had been a bad time. He'd never gone without in his childhood, not for the basic things anyway. So he couldn't share that experience with her.

He paused. "I never want you to feel that way, Kira. Ever again."

She swallowed. "Oh, Trace, I don't. You've always made me feel special. You've given me a great home and life here."

Then why did he feel like he'd let her down?

Two hours later, the barbecue was finished and the music had started just outside the barn on a portable dance floor that had been set up for the nighttime festivities.

Several kids were already dancing, including Jody. She looked adorable. For the next hour, the music switched back and forth between country and rock. When the country came on a lot of the parents made their way to the floor, showing up the kids with their two-stepping.

Cal and some of the ranch hands hung around playing chaperones, making sure the teenagers didn't go off by themselves. There had been strict rules for tonight's party, but that didn't mean some weren't going to try to break them.

She glanced around to see Trace talking with some of the fathers. So far he'd kept his distance since their meeting in the bathroom. Her breathing grew labored, recalling his near-naked body. All at once Trace looked her way. Their gazes locked momentarily, then someone called to her.

"Mrs. McKane."

Kira turned around to see Laura Carson hurrying toward her. "Have you seen Jody?"

"No, I thought she was with you."

The girl's eyes narrowed. "She was until Ben started bugging her. I left them alone because I was hoping they would talk and work things out." She pointed toward a group of trees. "The last time I saw them, they were over there, talking. Later, I saw Ben back with his friends but I can't find Jody anywhere."

"Did you ask Ben?"

She nodded. "He said he didn't know or care where she was."

Well, he was going to care. "Don't panic yet, I'll go look for her."

Kira was worried this would happen. She searched the area and ended up near Ben Kerrigan. She motioned for him to come to her.

"What's up, Mrs. M?"

"I'm concerned about Jody. I can't seem to find her. Would you know where she is?"

He shrugged. His gaze refused to meet hers. "Maybe she left."

"No, I was going to take her home later. I heard you two talked earlier. Was she upset about something?"

He glanced around nervously. "Maybe. We broke up a few weeks ago. She wants to get back together. I told her no way."

"Is that all you told her?"

He didn't say anything.

"At least tell me what direction she went."

"I don't know, maybe that way." He pointed past the corral.

Kira didn't say anything. She took off, knowing there was an upset girl out there, alone. Panic raced through her. She knew what that felt like.

Stopping to grab a flashlight from the barn, Kira headed through the empty corral toward the grove of trees. If Jody wasn't there she'd go back for help, but the last thing the girl needed was an audience for her humiliation.

She approached the trees and heard something. The soft sound of crying. Kira pointed the light toward the ground and kept walking. On a downed tree log, she found Jody. Her legs were drawn up and her head was on her knees, sobbing.

"Jody," Kira whispered as she approached.

The girl suddenly straightened and looked at her. "Who is it?"

"It's me, Kira McKane." She walked to her. "Are you okay?"

"Yeah, I'm fine." She stood and moved away. "Please, just leave me alone."

"I can't, Jody. And you're not okay. Let me help you."

She shook her head. "No! No one can help me. Everybody will hate me when they find out…" She started to walk away.

"No, Jody, they won't. I won't, I promise. I want to help, no matter what it is." Kira hesitated, trying to choose just the right words. "Let me help you."

"Why?"

"I understand what you're going through."

"No, you don't. Nobody does. And Ben doesn't care. He said he never cared about me. And now, he'll hate me."

"That's not true. He's just scared. So are you."

"What do you know about it?"

Kira took a breath and released it, catching movement by a tree. She tensed even more when she recognized the familiar silhouette. Trace. He stepped out so she could see his face in the moonlight. Luckily Jody couldn't.

"I know what it's like to feel alone," She continued to talk. "You think you have nowhere to turn, no one to trust enough to tell them you're pregnant."

She gasped. "How did you find out?"

This wasn't how she wanted Trace to learn about her past. Tears filled her eyes, praying he would understand. "Because I've been there, Jody. I was fifteen. And pregnant."

Trace froze, fighting to draw air into his lungs as he stared at his wife. Kira? Kira had a baby? In five years of marriage, she'd never told him.

"You're just saying that," Jody countered.

He tried to make out Kira's face in the moonlight. He heard the pain in her voice as her arms hugged herself.

"No, Jody, I'm not," she went on to say as she went to the girl. "And I felt exactly like you do right now. Alone. Like there's nowhere or no one to turn to. But there is, Jody."

The girl began to sob again. "No. My mother can't handle this. I. . .I let her down. Oh, what am I going to do?"

She took the girl's hands. "Jody, listen to me. You're not alone. There's help out there, and a lot of options for you."

Jody was quiet for a long time, then asked, "What happened to your baby?"

There was a long pause. "I gave him up." Kira's voice was raw with emotion. "I had no family to help me, and I was too young to keep him."

Jody looked up and started to speak—that was when she spotted him in the shadows. "Oh, Mr. McKane." She stumbled to stand.

Kira turned around, too. "Trace."

"Sorry to interrupt." He stepped further into the lit area. "I just wanted to make sure you were all right."

Kira went to him. "We're fine."

"That's good. Then I'll leave."

"No, we'll go back with you." She squeezed Jody's hand. "We'll talk more later. We'll deal with this together, Jody."

The girl nodded. "Thank you."

This time Kira had no doubt that Trace overheard her admission. Maybe it was better it happened this way. She wouldn't have to figure out a way to explain why she gave away her son. The guilt she'd felt every day since. And no matter what kind of absolution she got from him, it wouldn't make up for the loss she'd felt every day for almost fifteen years.

The night had finally come to an end as Trace watched the last of the graduates and their parents drive off.

Everyone had been exhausted from the day's events, but the roundup was completed successfully and the students had a great time at the party, not realizing what had gone on behind the scenes.

Trace looked at the house. He needed to talk to Kira. With everything going on at the party, there hadn't been time. He fought the anger building inside him. Though could anyone blame him? She'd kept a secret from him, a big secret.

He released a breath and walked up the back steps to the house. No matter how it ended up, it was time she told him everything about her past.

After sending Jake Peterson's dad off with the last of the tables and chairs, he walked into the kitchen and found Kira wiping off the counter. There wasn't much evidence left of the party. She finally turned around and met his gaze. "Oh, Trace. Is everyone gone?"

He nodded. "Yeah, it's just you and me. What about Jody?" The last he'd seen of the girl had been after they'd brought her back. She sneaked her upstairs until the party ended.

"Laura's parents took her home. I'm going by tomorrow to help her explain things to her mother."

Trace nodded, but he was barely holding it together. Why were they discussing mundane things when their marriage was hanging by a thread? And it was weakening quickly with the weight of the secret she'd kept from him. Just another thing she couldn't share with him

"Were you ever going to tell me, Kira?" When she started to speak, he raised his hand. "And no more excuses, you owe me the truth. In two days we have another visit from the adoption agency, and a birth mother."

She hesitated, then said, "I know you won't believe me, but I was planning to tell you tomorrow."

"Is that what you were talking about with Mrs. Fletcher when I walked in the nursery that day?"

She nodded. "She was going over my medical records, asking about miscarriages and live births. I didn't want to lie."

That did it for Trace. "But it's okay to lie to your husband."

"I didn't exactly lie, Trace."

"No, you just omitted something very important in your past."

"It was a painful past. I never shared that time with anyone. Can't you understand I wanted to forget, to start over," she pleaded. "I wanted a life with you."

He cursed and looked away.

Kira felt the familiar rejection shoot through her body, nearly crippling her. But somehow she found the strength not to let it show.

"Okay, Trace," she began. "What do you want to know? How I could give up my own baby? How could I let a boy talk me into sex at barely fifteen?" She glared at him. "Don't you know all foster kids are wild? We'll do anything." More tears flooded her eyes, blinding her. "I was no better than trash."

"Stop it," he ordered.

"Oh, but you want to hear the truth, don't you? Do you have any idea what it feels like to be an outcast, to have no friends?" She paced along the island counter, glad it was separating them. "It wasn't so bad in grade school, but by the time I was in high school, kids wanted nothing to do with me. Then Michael came along and gave me a little attention, and I grabbed it. Gullible me, I believed him when he said he loved me." A laugh escaped as she swiped at the tears on her cheeks. "Oh God, it had been so long since I'd heard those words. Then when I told him I was pregnant, he acted as if he didn't know me.

"I was devastated," she said in a hoarse whisper. "Worse, the father of my baby was my foster family's nephew. I was packed up so fast and shoved out the door, I didn't know what was happening."

"Where did you go?"

"Girls like me go into a group home. There were several of us who were pregnant. I stayed there until I delivered my baby. My little boy. But I couldn't keep him."

She tried to hold it together, but failed, covering her eyes she began to sob. Then she felt Trace's arms around her, holding her.

"I'm sorry, Trace. I know I should have told you. But I was afraid that you wouldn't want me either."

"Shh, Kira. Don't talk."

Trace couldn't stand to hear any more of her pain. What she had to go through alone. He was hurt by her lack of trust, but he understood why she'd kept the secret.

Why she desperately wanted another baby.

Kira lifted her head, pain etched on her face. "It's better now that it's out in the open. I was wrong to push you for a baby, Trace. I'm sorry for everything." She turned and hurried out of the room.

He was left dazed. She truly thought that he would leave her because of her past. Why not, everyone else had in her life. He wanted to go to her, but knew if he did he had to make the commitment he was staying, if not as her husband, at least as the father to a baby. He knew he wanted to be both he just didn't know how to make it happen.

A chill rushed through him at the thought of never having Kira in his life. He wouldn't have much of a life without her. The past few months had proven that. He made his way through the house, and when he reached the stairs, took them two at a time and nearly ran down the hall to their bedroom. The door was open and he looked inside to find Kira on the bed.

His chest tightened painfully. "Kira," he breathed.

She wiped her eyes and sat up. "Do you need some clothes?"

"No. I don't need any clothes. I came to see you."

Her blond hair was mussed, her brown eyes were searching for any encouragement from him.

His eyes watered and his throat tightened. "I wish I could have been there for you." He thought about the agony she must have gone through trying to fill that void in her life. "I understand why you want a baby so desperately." She had no family, except for a grandmother who hadn't wanted her and a child she hadn't been able to keep.

A son Kira had never been able to see grow up.

He came further into the room. Now, he understood so many things. And he loved her more for her strength to survive the cards life had dealt her.

"So you're going to leave me, too."

He swallowed. "It would be easier to forget to breathe. Do you have any idea how many nights I've lain awake in that damn bunk, thinking about you?

Thinking about the talking, the sharing, and about how we used to turn to each other in the night and how sweet it was to hold you in my arms. How loving you was heaven. How badly I wanted you."

Kira sucked in a breath, eager to hear every word, praying she wasn't dreaming.

He reached the bed, his gray gaze locked with hers, his voice husky with emotion as he continued, "It's been hell."

Kira's eyes searched his. "For me, too. I know I turned away from you and that hurt you."

He placed his finger against her lips. "No more talking, Kira. Not now." He leaned forward and brushed a kiss over her mouth. She froze as his lips slowly moved over hers, drawing feelings out that she hadn't acknowledged in so long.

She wanted Trace, and she knew he still wanted her. He broke off the kiss and studied her. "I want you, Kira. Don't push me away, not tonight."

"Oh, Trace, I won't." She wrapped her arms around his neck and kissed him, letting him know her desire. It wasn't long before they had stripped off their clothes.

Under the covers, Trace pulled her against his body and his hands moved over her. Soon he made her forget everything.

At least for a little while, everything was perfect between them.

CHAPTER SEVEN

AT DAWN the next morning, Kira opened her eyes to see the familiar surroundings of the master bedroom. And to the once familiar feel of Trace's body as she lay pressed against him. She shifted her gaze to his face relaxed in sleep.

She stared up at the ceiling and recalled every precious moment they'd shared. The few hours they'd stolen together. It had been like their first year of marriage before her obsession for a baby. Before Trace learned of her past. And it didn't solve anything.

Her eyes filled. After last night it was going to be harder to stay away from Trace, but she had to. If she wanted to survive giving him up, she had to find a way.

Trace stirred and instinctively drew Kira tighter against him. She forced herself not to react. She fell back into a doze waking again only when, she felt him move away and get out of bed. Slipping on his jeans, he pulled his T-shirt over his head as he walked out of the room.

Kira opened her eyes as her husband walked out of the bedroom, relieved that they skipped the-morning-after-talk. He'd probably gone off to do chores. She collapsed back on the pillow, trying not to think about their perfect night together. No matter how good they'd been together, it still hadn't changed anything. They had problems. And in the end, she still couldn't give Trace a biological child.

Trace stood in the kitchen trying to hold onto his common sense. A perfect night in bed with his wife didn't mean their marriage was back on track, but it was the closest they'd been in months. And he wanted this to be a new beginning for them. Although words weren't spoken, he knew she still loved him. He felt the same way.

He poured some coffee. But he couldn't help but have hope, hope that they could make it work between them.

He went to the refrigerator and took out the orange juice. After filling two glasses, he carried them to the table. There were two place settings already set out for their breakfast.

Kira walked into the room, wearing a floral satin robe. He immediately paused, registering she didn't have a damn thing on underneath. Great. Had she suddenly run out of clothes? He sucked in a long breath and released it.

"I thought we could use some coffee and a little sustenance," he informed her.

Kira went to the table and picked up a mug. She brushed her blond curls back from her face and took a sip. The fabric clung to every curve of her luscious body.

"Thank you," she told him.

He also savored the hot brew, letting the caffeine

kick-start him. Then he watched as she sipped from her mug, her big brown eyes locked on him. He could feel the tension.

"You want a sweet roll?"

"Maybe later," she said. "I think we should talk?"

He turned a chair around and straddled it. He didn't have much choice. "Okay, tell me what's on your mind?"

Kira joined him, sitting down across from him. "What happened last night wasn't planned." She held up her hand. "And I want you to know that I don't expect anything from you."

He tensed. "So we just used each other for comfort."

Her eyes widened. "Stop putting words into my mouth. A lot happened yesterday, and I turned to you because I trust you…and I care about you."

"And I care about you. Dammit, Kira. Do you think I can just turn off feelings after all these years."

"Right now, we're both too vulnerable to jump back into this." Kira knew she had to protect herself. "I think we should back up a little while."

"You mean for six months, until you get a baby."

She tried not to flinch. "I want to use the six months to see how we get along."

"And then you walk away."

She sighed. "No, so we can both rebuild our lives. I thought you agreed to this?"

"I agreed to meeting with the counselor. We're well past that."

"Okay, here's your chance. Tomorrow, we're possibly going to meet a birth mother who may choose us." She took a breath and released it. "That's hard to comprehend."

He remained silent and let her talk.

"I know it's happening quickly, Trace, but we need to make a decision." She set down her mug and looked at him. "I know you were blindsided yesterday when you learned about my baby, but it's something I can't change. So now, we have to decide if we move ahead."

He could hear the trembling in her voice. He wasn't too steady, either. He'd made a lot of mistakes in the past.

"There's nothing to forgive, Kira." He wished he could have been there for her. "And I know how much adopting a baby means to you."

Kira tried not to get too excited over Trace's words. "So you want to go along with it for…six months? To see how things work out."

She watched his eyes flare. "Your idea isn't foolproof, Kira. What happens if we don't get picked tomorrow?"

She'd be heartbroken. "I have to stay positive. I didn't want you to feel trapped, either."

"Trapped into what? We agreed to adopt a long time ago."

"We need to act as if we have a real marriage for the full time, Trace." She blinked back tears. "I don't want a man who walks out if things get tough."

"Isn't that what you're going to do, eventually?"

She ignored his sarcasm. "So are you moving back home?"

He paused. "I can't just jump back into it as if we never had problems."

"I know. That's why I'll be moving into the guest room."

"Like hell!"

She suddenly got hopeful.

"I'll sleep there."

She worked hard to hide her hurt. "If it's what you want?"

"Hell, no, it's not what I want." He shot up and marched to the window. "This isn't easy for me, Kira. And last night with you didn't help. I hate to fail. But if we're lucky enough to get a baby and that's no sure thing," he warned before shrugging. "Who knows, we might just get along."

Barely containing her excitement, Kira boldly walked over to Trace, raised herself up on her bare toes and brushed her mouth across his. Hearing his groan, she deepened the kiss and he quickly joined in. By the time she pulled back she could see the desire in his eyes. "That was to officially welcome you home." She turned and strolled off. Her husband needed something to think about on those lonely nights in the guest room.

A few hours later, heading into town, Trace was still wondering if he'd done the right thing by moving back into the house. Kira had gone to see Jody, and he needed to talk to his brother.

Since it was Sunday, Jarrett was at home. Trace drove to the custom-built home on the land that his brother had kept when he sold him the half of the ranch their parents had left him.

The two-story, modern structure sat on a hill with rolling green lawn in front, and the back overlooked a picturesque view of the mountain range. Trees lined most of the property, adding privacy to the large deck and hot tub.

Trace made his way along the blue stone walk and rang the bell. His brother quickly answered, dressed in jeans and a blue collared shirt.

"Hey, Trace, you made it. Come in."

"I said I'd be here." Trace stepped into the slate tiled entry, then into a huge great room with a stone fireplace that took up most of one wall. Oversize brown leather furniture made up a cozy seating area around the hearth. He followed his brother across the hardwood floors to the dining room, off a kitchen with black cabinets and marble countertops.

"Nice place."

Jarrett frowned. "You haven't been here before?"

"No. I guess my invitation got lost in the mail."

His brother ignored the comment. "You and Kira are always welcome anytime."

"I'll pass that along to my wife." He didn't care if he was added to Jarrett's social list or not. "Okay. So what do you want to talk to me about?"

"I have everything laid out here."

Trace turned and looked at the table. "What are you talking about?"

"The property deal."

He had contracts drawn up? "I never said I would sell, just that I'd talk to you."

Jarrett studied him. "Come on, bro, you know you can't come up with the payment."

Was his brother just waiting for him to fail? "You know nothing, *bro*. I have the money."

His brother motioned for Trace to take a seat, then he sat across from him. "We both know that the adoption costs could run to a sizable amount."

Trace didn't want to talk to Jarrett about this. "I'll take care of it."

"What if you can't? You could lose the ranch and the baby."

And Kira, he thought. "Okay, what's your plan?"

"Simple." Jarrett slid a paper across the table. "I want to buy back the section of the land that borders my property."

Trace didn't believe this was out of the kindness of his brother's heart. "We talked about this before, Jarrett. I don't want that land developed with homes."

"And I won't, not for ten years."

That made Trace suspicious, too. His brother didn't do anything that didn't benefit himself. Yet, did Trace have any other options? The past few years, they'd had a lot of expensive medical procedures for Kira, costs that the insurance hadn't covered, combined with two lean years of cattle profits. The money he'd held back for emergencies was nearly gone.

He glanced down at the property agreement. The balloon payment was due the end of June. Three weeks. He looked at his brother. Something told him not to trust him. There had been too many times his older brother had used him.

"Can you give me a week to think about it?" Trace asked.

Jarrett hesitated, then nodded. "That's about all I can give you."

Why was that important if his brother wasn't going to do anything with the land? He needed to think about this.

Jarrett nodded. "Also, I wanted to give you this card for Kira."

Trace took it. "Dr. Thomas Faulkner, Fertility Specialist."

"We knew each other in college and kept in touch. I told Kira about him."

Why the hell was Jarrett discussing anything with his wife?

"I thought she'd mention it to you."

Trace thought they'd exhausted every avenue on fertility. Besides, they were ending their marriage. He suddenly thought about the parting kiss she'd given him earlier. Between last night and this morning, it didn't feel like things were ending to him. "Did she say she wanted to get in touch with this doctor?"

Jarrett shrugged. "I don't think you should give up, Trace. That's another reason you should sell me back the land."

Trace didn't want to listen anymore. "I need to go. I'm meeting Kira for lunch," he lied.

Jarrett watched Trace. "Okay, but think it over…this is a good deal for you."

Trace knew from experience that wasn't true. His brother was up to something, and he was going to find out what it was.

Two hours later, Kira tried to hold on to the afterglow as she drove into town. Not just from Trace making love to her last night, but because he was moving back into the house, and agreed to the adoption. Okay, it was only to the guest room, and he wouldn't be around to be a daddy to her baby, but it was a start. A big one. Although he seemed angry about her dismissing their love making, at least they were talking again.

Kira sobered as she turned down Elm Street toward Jody's house. It wasn't the best neighborhood, bringing back memories of her own childhood. When she was a little girl, she remembered her parents had lived paycheck to paycheck, so when they'd died, there wasn't any extra money to help raise their only child. Just the little that her grandmother got, but the ailing woman decided not to take her granddaughter in.

Kira pushed away the bad memories and parked at the curb of the small rental house. The lawn needed to be mowed, and the house could use a fresh coat of paint. It amazed her that Jody could deal with all this and still make the grades in school. Kira was going to do everything she could to help her now.

She climbed out and went up the walk. Soon, the door opened and Jody greeted her. The teenager looked tired and worried.

"Hi, Mrs. McKane."

"Hello, Jody." She hugged the girl. "How are you feeling today?"

"Better now that you're here." Jody nodded toward the door. "My mom just got up. It's her day off so she sleeps in."

Kira knew she was making excuses for Marge Campbell. She'd bet that it was Jody who took care of things around the house, along with going to school and working a part-time job.

"We're going to deal with this together, Jody."

Tears flooded Jody's eyes.

Kira hugged her again.

"Jody, who are you talking to?" Mrs. Campbell came to the door. "Oh, Mrs. McKane. What brings you here today?" Dressed in an old chenille robe, the forty-plus woman pushed back her wild, bleached-blond hair. Years of hard living showed in her lined face.

"Hello, Mrs. Campbell. Sorry to bother you, but Jody and I want to talk with you."

Marge Campbell glanced back and forth between the two, then slowly opened the squeaky screen door. Inside, the living room was furnished with a faded print sofa and two mismatched chairs. Although the ashtrays had been emptied the place still reeked of cigarette smoke.

Jody directed her to the sofa. Once they were all seated, Kira exchanged a glance with Jody.

"If this is about Jody going away to college," the mother began, "it just isn't possible. I need my daughter here to help out."

"No, Mom. It's not about college. I'm pregnant," the girl blurted out.

"What?" Marge gasped. "You promised you wouldn't do anything. That you'd stay away from those boys." She jumped up from her seat. "Now, what are we going to do raising some kid's brat? I warned you this would happen." She wheeled around on her daughter. "Who did this to you?"

Kira stood. "Mrs. Campbell, please can't we sit down and talk calmly about what to do?"

"She's going to get rid of it that's what she's going to do. I'm not going to be saddled with another kid. I've been through that once. Never again."

Kira could see the hurt on Jody's face. "Your daughter isn't saddling you with anything. This is her decision to make. She can get financial help if she decides to keep the child."

"Well, she's not bringing the baby here. So she can just get out right now."

After his visit to Jarrett's place, Trace returned to the ranch, packed up his things from the bunkhouse and carried them up to the house.

Things were far from perfect, but he would deal with it. He only had to stay out of his wife's bed. Sure. He couldn't even stop himself remembering how willing she'd been in his arms last night. In the dark they didn't need words, just their bodies to express their need for one another. He'd never shared that level of intimacy with anyone but Kira. How could he live without her now?

That was the reason he was going to use this time to try to make things work. He might go crazy wanting his wife, but he had to think beyond his own needs; there could be a baby added to the mix. Maybe if he'd worked harder, instead of moving out, he'd have a wife, a lover. He couldn't leave her now, especially with the possibility of a baby. Not without a fight, anyway.

He'd finished putting his shaving kit in the bathroom when he heard the back door open. She was home. Good. Cal could handle the chores today, and he could spend the day with his wife. Just maybe he could convince her to change some of the rules. He hurried down the steps and went into the kitchen to greet her. He quickly stopped when he saw she wasn't alone, Jody Campbell was with her.

Kira saw him. "Oh, hi, Trace."

"Kira. Hi, Jody."

She shyly looked away. "Hello, Mr. McKane."

He turned back to a nervous Kira.

"Jody is going to be staying with us for a few days. Her mother was upset about the…news. So I brought her home to discuss options."

So they weren't going to be alone. Hiding his disappointment, he turned to his houseguest. "Welcome, Jody. You stay as long as you need."

"Thank you, Mr. McKane."

Kira turned to their guest. "Why don't you go upstairs and rest? The guest room is the door just past the nursery. We'll bring your suitcase up later."

The girl nodded and left the kitchen. Once alone, Kira released a breath and turned to her husband. "I guess I should have called, but Jody was literally out on the street." She frowned. "You sure you don't mind her staying here?"

He shook his head. "A few days won't be bad."

Kira grimaced, hoping Trace would understand. "It might be longer. Her mother didn't take the news of the baby well. I want to make sure Jody has some kind of support."

"What about the baby's father? Shouldn't he be here for her?"

"Jody said she tried to tell him, but he wouldn't listen."

"Maybe he'll listen to me," Trace said. "He's got to take responsibility."

"Ben leaves for the Army in a few weeks. He's not a bad guy, but he's a kid, and Jody will be eighteen next month." She shook her head. "Neither one of them are ready for this. I'm sorry, but when her mother threw her out, I just couldn't let Jody go through this alone."

He stepped closer, taking her hand. "She's lucky to

have you, Kira. I just had some plans for us today. I thought we could go riding."

"You wanted to take me riding?"

"You sound surprised. I thought we should practice getting along—since Mrs. Fletcher will be watching us."

Kira was thrilled Trace wanted to spend time with her. It had been so long since they'd done anything carefree. "Could I get a rain check?"

He nodded. "Seems we have another problem. I just moved my things into the guestroom." He raised an eyebrow. "Have any idea where I put them now?"

When Kira woke the next morning, smiling, she stretched her arms out. She reached across the big bed but Trace wasn't there. Not that she should expect him to be. Although he'd come to their room to give the appearance all was normal, after Jody retired for the night, he had gone to the bunkhouse. Since Trace was up before the sun, their houseguest wouldn't even suspect he wasn't sleeping next to his wife.

That hadn't stopped Kira from missing him. She better get used to it, though, because his absence was going to be a permanent feature soon enough. Trace was only playing the part of attentive husband.

Kira got up and headed for the shower to help her focus on her day. This afternoon Mrs. Fletcher was coming with a special visitor. And it could mean they'd have a baby by summer's end. Kira tried to hold in her excitement, but couldn't as she began singing in the shower.

Thirty minutes later, she went downstairs and found Jody doing the dishes.

"Good morning, Jody," she greeted her. "I hope you slept okay."

"Good morning, Mrs. McKane. I slept fine. The bedroom you let me use is so pretty."

"It is pretty, isn't it?" Kira smiled and went to the coffeepot and poured a cup. "I especially love the old iron bed. I found it in the attic." She sipped from her mug. "I'm sure glad that my husband's family didn't throw anything out."

"Your house is beautiful. I hope you don't mind, I dusted the living room. I can fix you breakfast if you want."

"Jody, I didn't bring you here expecting you to work."

"I just want to help out."

"I know you do," Kira said. "But I think it's more important that you see a doctor. Have you been to one?"

"I went to the clinic on Main Street just to confirm my pregnancy."

"How far along are you?"

"Fourteen weeks."

Kira sat down at the table and motioned Jody to do the same. "Have you thought about what you want to do?"

Jody shook her head. "Only that I can't end this pregnancy."

"What I told you, Jody, about me giving my baby up. It was the right decision for me, and the best for my baby. That doesn't mean it's what's right for you."

"I know that." Jody's gaze met hers. "I'm never going to tell anyone about what you told me."

"It's okay, Jody," Kira assured her. "I'm not ashamed of what I did. My baby was given a life I never could have offered. Two parents for one thing."

The girl looked thoughtful. "I don't know what I want to do."

"Well, we'll go to the doctor first. I'll set up an appointment for tomorrow. What time are you working today?"

Jody gasped. "I have the dinner shift."

There was no way Kira was going to miss Mrs. Fletcher. "I have an appointment here this afternoon, so you can take my car."

"I can't drive your car."

"Why not? You have a driver's license don't you? I trust you."

Tears filled the girl's eyes. "You've been so nice to me. I don't know what I'd do…if you hadn't took me in."

Kira hated to see the girl's lack of confidence, but she understood it. "You're easy to be nice to, Jody. Don't let anyone tell you anything different. And I'm going to stand by you for as long as you need me."

She knew too well what it was like to be alone, and pregnant. Maybe she could make a difference in Jody's life.

"They're here," Kira gasped.

Trace went to the kitchen window in time to see two women get out of the car. He recognized Mrs. Fletcher, but his attention went to the young girl with her. She was tall and slender, her stomach protruding with the late stage of pregnancy.

"Do I look okay?" Kira turned to look at Trace, brushing at her blue print sundress. Her wheat-colored hair was pulled away from her pretty face.

"You look perfect," he said truthfully. "Please, Kira, take a breath. She's going to like you. Remember, though, this is an interview. We might not even find out anything today."

He needed to stay calm, too. Mainly because he didn't want Kira disappointed if things didn't work out.

Her hand rested on his arm. "What about you, Trace? Are you sure this is what you want?"

He wanted whatever Kira wanted and a baby would be nice. "Yes, Kira, this is what I want. Now, we better go answer the door before they leave."

Together they walked to the back door and opened it as the two women came up the steps. "Hello, Mrs. Fletcher," Kira called.

The counselor smiled. "Trace, Kira, it's nice to see you again." She stopped on the porch to make the introductions. "This is Darcy Heaton. Darcy, this is Trace and Kira McKane."

"It's so nice to meet you, Darcy," Kira said and took her hand. The greeting was repeated by Trace to the girl in her late teens or early twenties.

"Hello," the girl said shyly. "You have a beautiful place here. I always wanted to live in the country."

"I could show you around if you want," Trace said. "We just finished the roundup this past weekend, and this morning shipped off the steers to the feedlot. But we have several horses."

Darcy's eyes lit up. "I love horses."

"Then let's go to the barn and I'll introduce you to Thunder."

Trace walked off with the young mother-to-be, followed by Mrs. Fletcher and Kira. Once inside the barn, he took Darcy along with him to see each animal. Thunder was willing to show off a little. Cal arrived with his mount, and Darcy was intrigued even more. They explained about the ranch operation, then Kira suggested they come into the house.

For the next hour, Kira found it easy to talk to Darcy as she and Trace showed her around the house. They sat down and had iced tea and cake while Darcy asked questions about the ranch. Then finally they ended up in the baby nursery. After a few moments Kira noticed that Trace and Mrs. Fletcher had wandered off, leaving her alone with the girl.

"This is a pretty room," Darcy said as she touched the cradle. "I like the yellow."

"Since I don't know the sex of the baby, I think it's a safe bet. But it's a good color to add pink or blue to."

Darcy nodded, eyeing the walls. "Do you want a boy or a girl?"

Kira couldn't help but wonder if this was a test. "Honestly, Darcy, it doesn't matter to us. We've tried everything for the last few years. We just want a baby to love."

Darcy nodded, then suddenly she looked sad. "I want to keep my baby, but I can't. My boyfriend, Wade, was in college." She hesitated. "He was so happy when he got the news about the baby. We were going to be married, but then, he was killed three months ago in a car accident coming to see me."

"Oh, Darcy." Kira fought to keep from going to her. "I'm so sorry."

A tear found its way down Darcy's cheek. "I can't raise my baby by myself. I have no family and it's important to me to know my baby will be loved and in a good home."

Kira felt a little shaky. "Your baby will be loved here. This home has seen several generations of McKanes. If you decide to let us raise your baby, he or she will be a McKane, too."

Darcy looked thoughtful. "I never had much of a home growing up, so it's important my little girl does."

Kira's heart tripped. "Your baby is a girl?"

"Is that all right?"

Tears filled Kira's eyes this time. "A little girl is perfect."

Just then Trace and Mrs. Fletcher walked into the room. He went to his wife's side. "Is everything okay?"

She nodded. "Darcy's baby is a girl."

Darcy went to Mrs. Fletcher. "I've decided."

The counselor sobered. "Are you sure, Darcy?"

"I'm sure." The pregnant girl placed her hand protectively on her stomach. "Trace and Kira, I want you to be the parents of my baby."

CHAPTER EIGHT

IN LESS than five weeks they were going to be parents.

The next evening, Trace glanced at Kira across the truck's bench seat as they rode into town. She hadn't stopped smiling since the announcement from Darcy. He wanted this for her, but it was all happening a little fast.

Just a few hours ago they'd all sat down at the kitchen table, Mrs. Fletcher laid out what Darcy would need. Top of the list was paying for the birth mother's medical bills. When the counselor gave him the approximate amount it nearly staggered him. Where was he going to get that kind of money? Thoughts of his brother's offer came to mind, but he quickly pushed them aside and turned his attention back to Kira.

Last week they were barely talking, now they were going to be parents. He let out a breath. No matter what she said about doing this on her own, he couldn't just walk away from her or this child. Somehow he had to figure out a way to keep her.

"Trace?" Kira's voice interrupted his thoughts. "Are you having second thoughts?"

"No, just a little overwhelmed."

He looked at his wife who was all dressed up for their night of celebration in town. Jody's idea and treat. Kira looked beautiful dressed in a silky blouse that outlined her full breasts, and a flowing skirt that hit the middle of her shapely calves. Even her feet looked sexy in a pair of high heeled sandals. She was distracting as hell. How was he supposed to live with her for the next six months, and not touch her, or kiss her?

"If it's the money, I planned to use the savings in the teachers' credit union."

Trace knew Kira had the account since before they'd married. He'd insisted it was hers. "I think you should hang onto it for now. I'll talk to Jarrett. He wants the southern section back. He'll pay well for it."

Kira turned toward her husband. "No, Trace. You wanted to keep that land, if just so he wouldn't develop it. Besides, I'm the one who asked you to do this."

He worked to control his anger. "We both wanted this adoption, Kira."

Tears welled in Kira's eyes. "Oh, Trace. You don't owe me this."

He pulled into the restaurant parking lot and shut off the engine. "Look, Kira, you already refuse to take anything from me, I sure as hell can at least help with this." And he was going to do a lot more whether she liked it or not. There was a child involved now.

Kira sat there staring out the windshield. She had hoped they could work this out, but Trace hadn't said much during the discussion with Lucy Fletcher. He hadn't expressed to her that he really wanted to be a family. Okay, she'd pushed him into this. And she hadn't a choice but to offer him a six-month deal.

If they couldn't make their marriage work, there would be a child involved then. At least this way, Trace could move on and have a family of his own.

She turned to him. "Thank you, Trace, for today. I promise I won't ask anything else from you."

"Ah, Kira." He reached for her and drew her against him. "You can ask me for anything."

She closed her eyes, reveling in their closeness, letting herself dream. The same dream she'd carried around since childhood. To have someone love her enough to always be there. She'd thought it was Trace, but in the end he would leave her like everyone else.

"We're going to make this work, Kira," he whispered in the darkness as he drew her closer. "You're going to have a baby."

Her heart gave a jolt as she raised her head. The truck was dark enough she couldn't see his eyes, but she felt them on her. "I wish I could be what you needed, too, Trace. I wish—"

Suddenly her words were cut off when he cupped her face and his mouth came down on hers. She only moaned as his lips coaxed hers until she gave in and opened so he could deepen the kiss.

He finally pulled back, his breathing labored and her hand felt the pounding of his heart. "Don't ever say that, Kira. You're everything a man could want."

"I couldn't give you a child," she managed to whisper.

He started to speak, but headlights from another car drew them apart. "We better go in," he said.

Trace climbed out of the truck and took the time to cool off as he walked around to the passenger side and helped her out. Their eyes locked in the dim parking lot. The mountain air hadn't helped—he wanted to kiss her again, then turn around and take her back home. Show her how much she meant to him.

Instead he escorted her toward the restaurant. Once inside the high-end steak house, Kira excused herself to go to the ladies' room.

"I'll check on our reservation," Trace said and went to the desk to speak to the young girl. "McKane."

"Oh, Mr. McKane. Your table should be ready shortly, Mr. Rhodes from EnRockies is waiting in the bar."

Trace quickly realized the girl's mistake; it wasn't the first time he'd been mistaken for his brother. Jarrett must be having a business meeting. "There must be a mistake. My wife and I have a reservation tonight. We're Jody Campbell's guests."

The young girl look flustered. "Oh, you're the other Mr. McKane."

Great. Now, he had the distinction of being the *other* brother. "I'm Trace McKane," he said as Kira returned to his side.

"Yes, here it is." The hostess smiled, embarrassed. "Your table is ready now, Mr. McKane." She called for a waiter, and he escorted them to a circular booth. Kira slid into the seat, and Trace was close behind her. After ordering cocktails, they were left alone.

Kira looked at him. "Is everything okay?"

He nodded. "Just a mix-up with the reservations. Seems Jarrett is here for a meeting."

"Wonder who Jarrett's wining and dining tonight."

Trace wondered, too. "Have you ever heard of a company called EnRockies?"

She frowned. "That's the name of the energy company drilling for natural gas in the area.

"Why would Jarrett be having a meeting with them?"

Kira shrugged. "Probably trying to lease them office space in town."

"Maybe." But an odd feeling gnawed at Trace. If the real estate business was so bad why would his brother want the land back? Something wasn't right.

"I can't believe he's looking to buy part of the ranch back."

"I don't want you to worry about it, Kira."

"How can I not? You could possibly lose part of the ranch."

"McKane Ranch is a big place. Dad meant for it to be divided between Jarrett and me, anyway."

Kira didn't look convinced. "That's great if he wanted to ranch, but we both know he'll develop the land if the price is right." Sighing, she leaned back. "I'm sorry, I shouldn't have said that. I don't know your brother that well."

"He's my *half* brother. And don't be sorry, Kira. It's true. I'm surprised Jarrett has stayed in Winchester Ridge. Of course he's made a good living being the hometown hero." A title he was all too familiar with having grown up in his older brother's shadow, the best quarterback to ever play at Winchester Ridge High School. "Who wouldn't trust him?"

Kira couldn't believe Trace could still be jealous of Jarrett. "He's a little too smooth for my tastes." She looked down at her husband's hands. His palm was rough from hard work, but could be so gentle, remembering his touch against her skin. "I prefer the rugged type," she continued, unable to stop herself. "A certain cowboy got my attention from the first day I arrived in town."

Trace's intense gaze locked with hers. "I guess I owe my brother for taking you to lunch." He leaned in closer to her. "That day I walked into the diner and saw you, you took my breath away." His voice turned husky. I don't have all the smooth words and moves, Kira. I'm just an ordinary guy who works hard to make a living."

It had always amazed her that he never knew the effect he had on people, on women. "Nothing about you is ordinary, Trace McKane."

He looked embarrassed.

She nodded. "I've made a lot of mistakes, Trace. You deserved to know about my past."

Her keeping that secret had hurt him, but he understood why she found it difficult to open up about it. He also knew how hard her life had been. The toughest part was knowing she had a child out there that she couldn't see. The only child she would ever give birth to. "I hated that you couldn't come to me."

The waiter dropped off their drinks, and asked for their order. Kira decided on the salmon, and Trace a steak. The waiter picked up their menus and left them alone.

Kira lowered her voice. "I know I should have trusted you, Trace. But at the time, I was made to feel ashamed about what happened, and the only way I could put it behind me was to bury it. I never planned on meeting you. When we started dating everything was so perfect. I was afraid I would lose you if you learned I gave up my baby."

Trace shook his head. "Like I said, Kira, that wouldn't have happened."

Kira still couldn't believe it—they were finally talking. Maybe if they'd managed it sooner, he'd be moving back into their bedroom, and not the guest-room.

She suddenly heard someone say her name.

Kira looked up to see Jody arrive at the table. "I'm glad you made it." The girl smiled, dressed in her uniform. A white Western blouse and black jeans.

"You didn't need to do this, Jody," she said.

"I know, but I wanted to thank you for letting me stay with you."

"You should be saving your money."

"I am. And I make good tips here. So order what you want—we get a discount on the food." She glanced over her shoulder, then back at them. "I better get back to my tables. Have fun." She hurried off.

"She looks so much better now."

Trace stared after Jody. "You've given her hope."

Kira turned her velvet-brown eyes to him. "So you don't mind her staying with us?"

"She's not around much to be a bother." Although he'd like to have more privacy with Kira. "Besides, she needs us."

She smiled. "Thank you."

He hated her acting like a stranger. "Hell, Kira, it's your home, too. It has been since the day I carried you over the threshold nearly five years ago."

She glanced away. "Things are different now."

He hated this time frame she'd concocted. "I don't want to be different, Kira. I can't walk away from the child, or from you. And I'll be damned if I'm letting you. Not if there's a baby involved."

The rest of their meal was eaten in silence as was their drive home. Kira wanted to talk about what Trace had said, but he'd clammed up.

Men.

They pulled up at the back door and she climbed out of the truck, not waiting for him. Well, she wasn't about to let him make a statement like that and refuse to explain.

They walked into the kitchen. "If you've changed your mind about the adoption, Trace McKane, you better tell me now."

"What makes you think that?"

"Maybe because you said you weren't going to walk away if there's a baby involved."

He glared at her. "That's true. You seem to think that I can sign papers, then turn around and walk out the door."

"No, *I'm* walking out the door," she corrected. "The baby is the only thing I'm taking." She never let herself feel the ranch belonged to her. "This is your place, your land."

"Dammit, Kira. That's what I mean. Why can't you believe me? I don't want you or the baby to leave."

Her breath stopped as she replayed his words. But before she could speak the sound of a car distracted her. Soon Jody walked into the dimly lit kitchen. "Hi. You guys home long?" She smiled.

"No, not long," Kira said. "Thank you again for dinner."

"Yeah, thanks, Jody. Now, we all need sleep," Trace

said as he locked the back door, then came back and took Kira's arm, leading her through the house to the stairs. Jody followed.

Kira's heart raced as they made their way down the hall and Trace opened the master bedroom door. "Good night, Jody," he called to her.

"Good night," the girl called as she went to her room.

Once Jody was out of sight, Trace pulled Kira across the threshold and closed the door behind them. He pushed her back against the raised wood panels. The room was dark, but she could feel his rapid breathing on her face.

"Let me turn on a light," she said, wanting to move away.

"No, Kira. It's better like this." He sighed. "I have something to say to you."

She shut her eyes tightly and began to pray. "Please don't say you're not going through with the adoption."

"No, I wouldn't do that. It's just not going to be your way. I want to negotiate a new deal. I want to be a father to this baby girl…and I want to be a husband to you." There was a long pause. "With no time limit."

Kira's chest tightened. "What if it doesn't work?"

"Then it won't be because we didn't try hard enough." He leaned forward and brushed his lips across hers.

She gasped. "Our track record isn't good, Trace." She slipped her arms around his neck, knowing she couldn't let him go.

"At least we'd have tried." He kissed the side of her neck as his arms wrapped around her waist. "And I want to try with you, Kira. And for this baby."

His mouth found hers in the dark as if a magnet drew

them together. The kiss grew intense along with their need, a need that hadn't diminished in their long months apart.

"Oh, Trace," she breathed as he broke off the kiss. She tried to come up with more resistance, but she was weak.

"Trust me, Kira." He tugged on her arm and together they walked to the bed. Slowly he began taking off her clothes, but she soon grew impatient and helped the process along, then did the same for him.

As she lay down on the mattress Trace leaned over her, his hands working their magic on her body, stealing her breath away, along with any doubts.

"We'll make this work, Kira."

Hope sprang inside Kira. Was this really going to happen? Was she finally getting her wish? A family.

A blissful three days and nights had passed, and Kira woke every morning, smiling. Trace had been a wonderful, attentive, considerate lover since the night they…renegotiated their marriage. Of course they had to steal their time together around their houseguest. But that was good practice for when their own child was here.

She walked into the kitchen to find Jody at the stove, cooking bacon. She glanced at the clock to see it was only seven o'clock. She told Jody repeatedly she didn't need to fix breakfast, but the girl kept doing it anyway.

"Jody, you should sleep in since you worked late last night."

The girl turned around. "Oh, Mrs. McKane. It's okay, I usually get up early."

Kira went to the coffeepot and poured a cup. "But you need your sleep, too."

The teenager's coloring had looked better this past week. "I'll rest later. I want to help out." The girl studied her for a while. "I don't want you to worry that I'll still be around when your baby comes. Cal is helping me figure some things out."

Jonas had been helping her? "Have you heard from your mother?"

Jody shook her head. "I don't expect to."

It was sad that her mother couldn't be there for her. But the baby's father needed to take responsibility, too. "Jody, have you told Ben you're pregnant?"

The girl took the bacon out of the skillet. "No. I tried at the party, and I've called, but he won't talk to me."

"He needs to know about the baby."

Jody turned around, tears in her eyes. "That's what Jonas says. But Ben will hate me."

Kira understood that feeling; she'd been there herself. "Ben has no cause to hate you. He helped make this baby."

"And he needs to take responsibility."

They both turned to see Trace and Cal standing at the doorway. They walked in and Trace came to Kira and kissed her, then turned to Jody. "If Ben won't listen to you, I think I should talk to him."

The girl blinked in surprise. "You don't have to do that, Mr. McKane."

"Someone has to. It's time for him to man up," Cal spoke up. "When does he go off to the Army?"

"In a few weeks."

"Then there's time," Trace said. "We'll drive you into town today." He rubbed his hands together. "Now, how about some breakfast? I'm starved."

"Me, too," Cal added.

Jody beamed. "I just need to cook the eggs. Is scrambled okay?"

The two men nodded. "That's our very favorite," Cal answered.

The teenager went to work, Cal went to get coffee, and Trace sat down at the table. He winked at Kira as she joined him.

She smiled in return. "Thank you for standing up for Jody. I don't think many people have."

"I'm just practicing for when we have our daughter."

It had been getting easier for Kira to believe. That she and Trace were going to be parents. A child together. "So you don't mind that the baby's a girl?"

"Mind having two beautiful women in my life? I don't think so."

She gripped his hand. Things were getting better every day. "I think we're pretty lucky, too."

After chores Trace and Kira drove Jody into town to see Ben. He glanced in the rearview mirror of the SUV and saw the nervous teenager in the back seat. A strange protectiveness came over him.

"Jody, it's going to be all right. Ben just may surprise you."

Jody nodded. "I think he suspects already. I think that's why he's been avoiding me."

Trace looked at Kira, then turned onto Ben's street. After finding the right house, he parked in front. "Well, that's going to end now."

"Do you want us to go with you?" Kira asked.

Jody shook her head. "No. I need to tell him by myself." She climbed out of the car and walked to the door.

"Are you sure we should let her go on her own?" Trace said, watching Jody.

"I think she wants to hear what he has to say." Kira sighed. "I hope she doesn't have any delusions that they're going to get married and raise this baby."

Trace glanced at Kira. "This has to bring back bad memories for you."

She shrugged. "Teenage girls at that age want love."

"And teenage boys are only after sex."

Kira kept her gaze on the house as she swallowed. "In the end everyone gets hurt."

Just then Jody came running out the front door. She climbed into the back seat and wiped at the tears streaming down her face. "Please, just go."

"What happened?"

"Ben doesn't want anything to do with the baby. He said it wasn't even his, and just to get rid of it." She sobbed. "It is his, Mrs. McKane. I loved Ben. There's never been anyone else."

Trace fought his anger as he climbed out of the car and marched up to the house. He rang the bell, but got no answer. So he began pounding until finally Ben came to the door.

The teenager stood eye to eye with Trace in height, but was about twenty pounds lighter. He looked shocked and a little frightened to see who was on the porch. "Mr. McKane."

"That's right, Ben. Let's see how you handle what I have to say."

His gaze went to the car, then back at Trace. "If it's about Jody—"

"You're damn right it's about Jody. And your child.

The girl didn't get pregnant on her own. She came to ask you to help, and you humiliated her by saying the baby wasn't yours."

"Well, how would I know, she could have been with someone else."

"Do you honestly believe Jody would lie to you?"

The boy glanced away as he shook his head. "No. But I can't have a kid. I'm going into the Army."

"What about Jody? She applied to college. Instead she's going to be raising a baby."

The boy didn't say anything.

"As least think about what Jody is going through. Help her decide what to do. If she does decide to keep it, are you going to be a part of the baby's life? I guess what I'm trying to say is act like a man. If you're man enough to join the Army, you should be man enough to accept your responsibilities." He turned, stormed off the porch and back to the car, knowing he'd taken on the job of Jody's protector for the long haul.

All he could think about was no one had been there for Kira.

Two days later, Trace rode out to the land that was soon—if he couldn't find any money—going to be Jarrett's. He pulled up on the rein, and just sat back in the saddle. He'd always loved this area covered in rows of birch trees. It was prime property that Jarrett had initially wanted for himself. But at the time, his brother had wanted the money for another project and the home he wanted to build. That had been when they'd struck the deal.

Trace had agreed to a five-year plan to pay Jarrett for

the property. The land he'd thought to use for raising a herd of free-range beef. He needed a few years to prepare the grazing land, and to put up fencing to keep the cattle in the allotted area. There would be a lot of up-front expenses, but in the long run the payoff would be worth it.

Ranchers these days had to have numerous business ventures to keep afloat. He'd thought about following his neighbors and opening some land to hunters, maybe building some cabins to rent. That, too, took capital. And he didn't have any right now.

So maybe what he had to do now was make sure that the McKane Ranch would be around for future generations. That meant selling this prime section back to his brother.

There were other priorities now. Kira, and the baby that would arrive in just weeks. Oh, boy. He sucked in a long breath. Getting used to the idea took some doing.

A girl. Would she like to ranch? Maybe not. It was a hard life. But who was to say they couldn't adopt more children? Whoa! Slow down, man. She wasn't even born yet.

His thoughts turned to Kira. They'd come a long way in the last few weeks. He'd been welcomed back into their marriage bed. More importantly, he'd managed to convince her he wanted to be a part of her and the baby's future.

He smiled, thinking about Kira back at the house already adding pink paint to the walls in the nursery. And maybe he should help her.

Trace pulled on Thunder's reins to turn and started back to the house when through the trees he spotted a vehicle. He rode toward the property line that separated his and Jarrett's land and saw what looked like a survey crew marking off areas.

They stopped when he rode up. "Excuse me, is there something I can help you with?"

"Hello, Mr. McKane, I presume. Trace McKane?"

"That's me.

The man walked closer. "It's nice to finally meet you, Mr. McKane. I'm Frank Rhodes and this is John Thompson. We're from EnRockies and we're doing a survey."

There was that name again. What was Jarrett up to? It was still his property. "You do know that this is my land. I never agreed to any survey."

Frank Rhodes frowned as he exchanged a glance with John Thompson. "Mr. McKane, I was assured that you'd already okayed us having access to this section."

"By who? I hold the deed to this land." At least he did until he couldn't make the balloon payment.

"Jarrett McKane. He said he'd talked to you."

Trace felt the anger building. "About what?"

"About leasing the mineral rights under your land."

"What the hell?"

Rhodes hurried on to say, "It's directional drilling, Mr. McKane. There won't be a drilling tower on your land at all. EnRockies has always followed the strict guidelines of the Bureau of Land Management to protect the environment. If there are any more concerns, I assure you we will answer any questions."

"I have one big one. My brother. He never told me about any lease." Trace thought back to Jarrett's eagerness to buy back this land. That wasn't going to happen now. "Do you think you could come by the house in a few hours? I'd like to discuss this at length."

"We would be happy to. I'll give Jarrett a call, too. I want to get this settled."

Thunder shifted away. "Believe me, it's going to be settled once and for all."

CHAPTER NINE

Two hours later, Kira stood in the nursery and eyed her handiwork. The light pink vertical stripes below the white wainscoting looked great. This was definitely a little girl's room.

She also had her eye on a white Daisy Garden crib she'd spotted in the shops. The bedding had pink and yellow colors with a floral design. It was an extravagant purchase, but Trace was fine with her using the money in the credit union, so she didn't mind borrowing a little from it.

Excitement raced through her. She was going to be a mother. All these years of dreaming, praying for a baby and now it was going to happen.

As much as she wanted the experience again of a baby growing inside her, she was already in love with this little baby. She planned to do everything possible to bond with this child, to welcome Jenna Margaret into the McKane family.

The door slammed downstairs, bringing Kira out of her reverie. So Trace had come home to help her with the painting. She smiled and headed down to the kitchen, thinking how nice it would be to have her husband around once again. She reached the kitchen, but no Trace. She tracked him down in the office, bent over the desk going through files.

"Trace, is something wrong?"

He didn't even look up at her. "There's plenty wrong. I found a survey crew in the south section. The land I was going to sell back to Jarrett."

"Who was doing the survey?"

"EnRockies," he said, then filled her in on the rest of the story.

"No, Jarrett wouldn't do that to you." She'd always believed there was good in her bother-in-law.

"You're defending him?"

"I'm not, but why would he do this behind your back?"

"Money. It's not enough he's leasing them his own land, he wants more. Mine." He slammed a drawer. "Forget that, he has no regard for my feelings about drilling on McKane land."

Kira had only known what she'd heard in town, from students who had parents employed by this company. There seemed to be more positive than negative about EnRockies.

"I think you should listen to what they have to say."

Trace stared at Kira. She didn't understand, this was a bond he'd shared with his dad. Their love of the land. "Dad trusted us to protect the ranch. And by the looks of it with Jarrett, I'm going to have to do it on my own."

"Trace, I want to help you, too. All I ask is that you calm down and find out more information."

How could he stay calm when he could lose everything? "Why? It's not going to change my mind, Kira." He frowned. "And since when have you cared about the ranch? You've been wrapped up in other things."

His words hurt her. "I've always cared, you just chose to exclude me."

An hour later, Mr. Rhodes arrived at the house. Kira came into the room and introduced herself. She refused to be shut out of the meeting. If they were going to make their marriage work, she needed to be a part of everything, and that included the ranch operation. She listened to the lease offer and bit back a gasp when Mr. Rhodes quoted the amount of money that would be paid out monthly.

She tried to read the map of the area, telling them where they had drilling towers located. How the Bureau of Land Management and the state of Colorado had approved the project.

"Like I stated earlier, Mr. McKane," Rhodes began, "there won't be any tower on your property."

"But close," Trace challenged. "Close enough to the Roan Plateau."

"It's no secret you and your brother's properties are prime locations, but the drilling can be done by one tower, which Jarrett has already agreed to place on his property."

Kira watched her husband struggle to remain calm. So she came up with a question. "How long is your company's lease for, Mr. Rhodes?"

"It varies, Mrs. McKane, but when we leave, the land is left just like it was before we began drilling. We plan to do everything possible to protect the environment and that includes the wildlife. So that means we have to proceed slowly and cautiously in selecting locations around the plateau's base."

Suddenly there was a knock on the back door and Jarrett walked into the kitchen. He glanced around the table. "Looks like you started without me."

"You got that wrong, brother. You started a long time ago and left me out altogether."

Mr. Rhodes stood. "I'll leave you all to hash this over. We'll talk again. Here's my card. You can reach me anytime." He nodded to Kira. "Mrs. McKane."

Kira let their guest walk out on his own. She wasn't about to leave the brothers alone.

Trace spoke first. "Were you ever going to tell me?"

"Why? You'd just reject the idea."

"So instead you tried to take away my land and go ahead when you know how Dad would have felt about this?"

"The ranch will still be here, Trace. Besides, Dad gave us the ranch."

"But you never wanted to work it."

"Is it so hard to believe that I don't want to work eighteen hour days and never know if you'll make enough to live on?"

Kira was steamed by her brother-in-law's arrogance. She wouldn't blame Trace if he threw Jarrett out of the house.

"I do just fine," Trace argued. "Making money isn't all that makes a person happy."

"That may be all right for you. I want a better life and the lease will guarantee that."

"It also doesn't mean I have to go along with it."

"Fine. But you're going to lose the land anyway.

Word is you don't have the money to pay off the loan, Trace. That means it comes back to me. I'd say I win either way." He grinned. "Once again I'll come out on top, little brother."

Kira could only watch the scene unfold like a bad movie. She wanted to help her husband, but knew he wouldn't appreciate it. Trace had to handle this his own way.

"I have other ways to get my hands on the money."

Jarrett smiled. "It's just a matter of time before you can't keep up the ranch. You'll be borrowing until there's nothing left."

"Get out of my house, Jarrett. And don't come back."

Jarrett looked at Kira. "Call if you need anything."

She couldn't believe the nerve of the man. "You'd be the last person I'd call." She moved closer to her husband. Jarrett finally turned and left.

"I'm sorry, Trace."

Trace stiffened when Kira touched him. He pulled away and walked to the back door. "I need to get out of here."

"Trace, wait," she called to him. "Let me help."

He glared at her. "You can't, Kira. I'm about to lose everything."

Kira felt a pain deep in her chest, making it hard to breathe. He said "I" not "We." Like so many times before when it came to the ranch, she'd been excluded from his life.

Trace couldn't think clearly so he stalked out to the barn. A long, hard ride on Thunder was safer than getting behind the wheel of his truck.

Inside, he went into the tack room where he found Cal. With a nod, he grabbed a bridle and his saddle.

"I'm going for a ride." He walked out into the barn.

Cal followed him. "What's going on, Trace?"

"Nothing, I just need to get away."

"I saw the EnRockies' truck and Jarrett's car. I take it the meeting didn't go well."

Trace lifted the saddle onto the stall railing, opened the gate and went inside. "Yeah. My brother's trying to pull a fast one." He went on to explain the situation to his foreman.

"I have to admit, the man doesn't let anyone get in his way. What are you going to do about it?"

He slipped the bridal on Thunder. "No way is Jarrett getting the land back."

"Good. So you're talking a deal with EnRockies?"

Trace blew out a long breath. "It goes against everything Dad wanted."

Cal hung his arms over the railing and watched Trace saddle the horse. "Your daddy isn't here. He didn't have the problems you're facing, either. If you want to run a cattle operation, plus stop Jarrett, you'll need capital."

Trace looked at his friend. He'd earmarked most of his savings for the adoption. "What do you expect me to do?"

Cal raised a hand. "You have options, Trace. You can borrow the money from me. Or you can sell off your breeding bulls, or look over EnRockies' proposal. It might not be that bad."

Trace began running some of the things Rhodes had said through his head. "They want to do directional drilling onto my land." He tightened the cinch and dropped the stirrup in place. "The drilling tower and roads go on Jarrett's side of the property. I can't stop that."

"I think a lot of the reason this bothers you so much is because your brother's involved. Right there it seems shady." Cal was quiet for a moment, then said, "What does Kira think?"

Trace shrugged. "It doesn't involve her."

"It sure as hell does. She's your wife."

He didn't want a lecture. "I know that." He led his horse out of the stall. It was all a mess.

Cal went after him. "Come on, Trace, don't get all stubborn about this and close up."

Trace turned and glared at his friend.

The foreman backed off. "Okay, one thing at a time. At least ride over to Joe Lewis's place. They drilled on his ranch last year. It seems to me it would be nice to have extra money coming in every month to ease your worries, even help start up those projects you've always wanted."

Kira had suggested the same thing. Trace stopped outside the corral. "What, are you moonlighting for the energy company?"

"No, I'm just a friend who doesn't want you to lose everything. I know what this place means to you, but even if you lose it all, don't lose Kira. You two love each other."

Three hours later, Trace still wasn't back and Kira wasn't sure what to do. Kira was both angry and worried. How dare Trace just walk out. What did she expect? He'd done it before.

She marched into the office. This had always been

Trace's domain, but no more. She began to go through the financial files and found the ranch account. It had a pretty hefty balance after the selling of the calves. Yet, she also knew that the land payment was coming due. She went to the accounts payable and scanning the pages discovered the last payment was due to Jarrett at the end of June.

Kira gasped, seeing the considerable amount. This would pretty much wipe them out. How would they survive if she wasn't going back to work in the fall? And there were the adoption costs and Darcy's medical bills.

"What are you doing?"

Kira jumped and looked toward the doorway to see Trace. Why did she feel so guilty? "Since you wouldn't share the facts with me, I was seeing how much we owe Jarrett." She stood. "I had no idea it was so much."

He walked to the desk. "The payments over the years were reasonable, but the balloon is due."

"You should have told me, Trace."

His gaze held hers. "I was handling it."

Kira felt the tightness in her chest as he continued to push her away.

"Besides, we haven't exactly been on speaking terms in the past few months."

Another dig that hit hard. "There's money in the credit union. You can use that."

Trace shook his head stubbornly. "At this point it wouldn't do any good. That's your money anyway."

"No, it's ours."

There was a long silence, then Kira spoke up, "Trace, maybe we should sit down and talk with Mr.

Rhodes. You didn't get the chance to listen to the stipulations about the mineral lease."

Trace didn't hide his tension. "This is a cattle ranch, Kira. It has been for three generations."

She started to speak, but he stopped her. "I need to handle this."

Trace's dismissal hurt her. If she hadn't known before, she knew now, he didn't want her to be a part of his life.

Over the next few days, Kira wasn't encouraged about her relationship with her husband. Trace spent his evenings in the office. He hadn't even made an effort to come to bed until late. Their magical nights together, their promises of a future together seemed like a fleeting memory.

She had hoped that their bedroom would be a place where they reached out for each other, to share things, to work on renewing their commitment to each other.

But Trace had turned away from her.

Breakfast time hadn't been much better. Even Jody was uncomfortable around them. So when the teenager needed a ride to work, Kira offered eagerly to get out of the house.

Kira drove the car up to the highway toward town.

"Mrs. McKane…" Jody began.

"It's time you called me Kira."

The girl smiled. "Kira. Ben asked me to marry him."

This was a shock to Kira. "Oh, my. So you two have been talking, a lot." There had been nights she'd heard Jody crying. She'd comforted her, but knew she had to work through things herself. "Have you decided on what to do?"

"Not marry Ben for one thing. We're too young." Her voice lowered. "And he doesn't love me. Besides, Ben wouldn't be around. He'd be in the Army, and I'd be here alone."

"So you've decided to raise the baby yourself?"

The girl sighed. "I don't know yet. But I know I need a place to live."

"You're welcome to stay with us for as long as you like." Crazy since Kira was beginning to wonder where her home would be, but she would take Jody with her.

The girl shook her head. "No, that's not fair to you or Mr. McKane. So Cal is helping me find a place. My boss at the steak house has been wonderful. He says I can stay on as long as I'm able to work."

"That's good. It's still going to be hard, though. So please stay at the ranch, at least until the baby is born."

"I'm hoping not too long. Cal's got an idea where I can live cheap. The place will need some repairs, but he's offered to do them."

Seemed Cal had taken Jody under his wing.

"I can help paint and Cal said there's some furniture there," the girl said excitedly. "And I can get my bed from my mom's house. I paid for it anyway."

Kira glanced away from the road to Jody. "Sounds like you've thought about this."

"You and Mr. McKane have been wonderful to let me stay with you, but I can't anymore. I should be paying you rent. And I still need to get a car, but I have some money saved. Because I'm a single mom, I can get some help with my medical bills. And Ben's going to help out."

Kira smiled. Jody had always been an organized

student. This shouldn't surprise her. She drove into the restaurant parking lot. "What about your mother?"

"I'll be eighteen soon, so I don't have to ask her anything. Besides, she's moving away." The girl lowered her head. "Seems I've embarrassed her."

Kira parked the car. "If you were my daughter, I'd be so proud of you. You have a lot to handle for someone so young."

"You were young, too, Kira, when you had your baby," Jody said and hesitated. "Do you think you made the right decision? I mean giving your baby up?"

Kira still felt the emptiness; she always would. "I'll always feel the loss. But yes, I gave him a chance at a better life, better than I could give him. It wasn't easy, but it was the only way for me."

Jody smiled. "I'm glad you're getting a baby now."

"So am I."

"Thanks for bringing me to work. I'm going to spend the night with Laura, and she'll bring me back to the ranch tomorrow."

"Good. I'm glad you're hanging out with your friends. Have fun and I'll see you tomorrow."

Jody grabbed her overnight bag and got out of the car. Kira watched her go inside, then she pulled out of the parking lot. She headed across town to the teacher's credit union. Her stubborn husband refused her help, so she was taking matters into her own hands.

An hour later, she'd finished filling out the loan application and was told she'd get an answer in a few days. With renewed resolve, she headed back to the ranch. She knew Trace would probably be upset, but she couldn't let his pride take everything from him.

When she pulled into the driveway she was surprised to find Mrs. Fletcher waiting for her. She climbed out of the car and walked over to the counselor.

The sad smile on Lucy Fletcher's face caused Kira alarm. "Hello, Kira."

"Mrs. Fletcher. Is something wrong?" Oh God, please, no. Her anxiety grew. "Is Darcy okay?"

"Darcy is fine and so is the baby." She glanced around. "Is your husband here?"

"I'm not sure. Do you need to speak to him?"

Mrs. Fletcher hesitated. "Could we go inside?"

Okay, this wasn't good. They walked up the steps together and went into the kitchen. "Please, tell me why you came all this way."

"I have some news." She sighed. "Darcy got a call from her boyfriend's mother. It seems that she never knew about Darcy until she went through her son's things." A long pause. "She's offered to help Darcy raise the baby."

Kira's heart stopped as she sank into a kitchen chair. "Is she serious?"

"Yes, I checked it out." Mrs. Fletcher sat, too. "When Marion Clark learned about the baby she contacted Darcy and begged her to come live with her. Darcy agreed. Together they're going to raise the baby. With her son's death, Marion wants a part of him."

A tear found its way down Kira's cheek. She hated this, but deep down she understood. If there had been someone to support her, she would have kept her son, too. "I'm glad Darcy has someone to help her."

"I'm so sorry, Kira." Mrs. Fletcher took hold of her hands. "Darcy was adamant about finding a home for her child. She wanted you and Trace to raise her baby." She paused. "There was always a chance the mother could change her mind."

"I know." She was numb.

"I assure you, you and your husband are back on the list."

Another list. Her time had run out on her having a family with Trace. Kira stood. She couldn't talk anymore. "Thank you for everything, Mrs. Fetcher."

"You're welcome, Kira. I'll be in touch." She walked to the door. "Goodbye."

Kira didn't speak, she just walked upstairs to the nursery. She ran her fingers along the new crib and the dresser that had arrived just yesterday. She looked at the wall where the name JENNA was spelled out in large ceramic letters.

There was no baby girl.

She'd never felt so alone. So lost.

CHAPTER TEN

TRACE had taken Kira's advice and that afternoon drove over to see his neighbor, Joel Lewis. Together, they saddled two mounts and rode out to the EnRockies' drilling tower. The energy company had built an access road across the Lewis's pasture, but that was the most noticeable change. The high tower was partly hidden by the tall pines.

"It's not bad," Joel said as he leaned forward against the saddle horn. "I mean I had concerns at first, but in this day and age, farmers and ranchers need all the help they can get." The longtime neighbor looked at him. "I'm sure my daddy and yours would have raised a stink, but it's a different world now."

Trace couldn't help but think of all the money he owed, and how much easier it would be to have some extra income. "So you're okay with this arrangement?"

He nodded. "The extra money comes in handy when you have two college-aged kids, or when the wife needs a new car. We even took a vacation last year and started a retirement fund."

Trace thought about his parents and their struggles

running the cattle operation. He looked ahead to his own future. Would it be with Kira and the baby?

The sound of Joel's voice broke into his thoughts. "You've got it easy with your lease offer," he began. "It's Jarrett's property that's going to house the tower and handle the truck route. They're only going to do directional drilling onto your property. What's to think about?"

Trace sighed. "I guess I was just wondering what my dad would do."

Joel nodded. "It's your place now and you're the one fighting to keep it." He glanced around. "Where else could we live and enjoy this incredible backyard? Besides, I wouldn't survive in the city, nor would have wanted to raise my sons there. Have a couple of your own kids, Trace, and you'll change your mind quick."

It suddenly hit Trace. He had to think about his responsibilities to Kira, and the child. No matter what the original arrangement, he was definitely committed to the roles of husband and father.

This energy lease could help secure their financial future so he could continue to ranch. And so much more. Kira wouldn't have to work. He thought back to the past few days and his avoiding her. He needed to let her know how much he wanted her to be a part of his life, to include her in this decision.

Suddenly he couldn't wait to get home to talk to her about this.

"Thanks, Joel. You've helped a lot."

"Good. And if need be, I'll take Rocky off your hands."

They turned their horses back toward the barn. "Afraid not, Joel, that bull is going to be too busy, but I'd be happy to sell you one of his calves."

"Sounds like you're in the ranching business for a long time."

"What can I say? It's in my blood." He thought about the baby coming soon. "I plan to stay here to see another generation take over." And he was going to do everything he could to convince Kira to stay by his side for a lifetime.

Thirty minutes later, he pulled his truck up beside the barn and headed toward the house to talk with Kira. If they were going to make their marriage work, he needed to listen to her. He'd made it to the back porch when he heard Cal saluting him.

The foreman caught up to him. "I was wondering if you have any plans for the old foreman's cottage?"

Trace frowned as he looked past the new bunkhouse to the small house that had been abandoned for years. "It's just storage for my parents' stuff." He looked at his friend. "Why, did you want to move into it?"

Cal shook his head. "No, Jody needs a place to live."

Trace hadn't figured their houseguest was staying much longer. "Isn't she going home to her mother?"

Cal shook his head. "Her mother's leaving town. Jody hasn't any other place to go."

"She's leaving her daughter?"

"Jody will be eighteen next week. Her mother doesn't want to be saddled with a teenager with a kid. She's moving on with her new boyfriend."

Trace couldn't help but think of Kira at that age. There hadn't been anyone for her, either. "The cottage must be in bad shape."

"Not so bad. There's some water damage in the

bathroom, but I can fix that. And a good cleaning would help a lot."

"I don't want Jody living out there until it's fixed up," Trace said. "And I'm sure there's plenty of furniture in the attic to furnish the place."

"Thanks," Cal said. "Now, the biggest job will be to convince her to stay."

"I'm sure Kira can manage that." Trace started backing away. "Speaking of Kira, is she in the house?"

Cal nodded. "She came back about an hour ago. That Mrs. Fletcher was here, too. She didn't stay long, though."

Trace tried to remember if the counselor was scheduled to come by. Had he missed a visit? If so, why hadn't Kira called him? He hurried into the house.

"Kira," he called. The only sound was the refrigerator clicking on.

He walked through the house to the staircase. Taking the steps two at a time, he felt his pulse drumming in his ears as he reached the second floor, then down the hall. She wasn't in the bedroom, then he heard a noise in the nursery. He pushed open the door and found Kira on the floor. With a screwdriver in hand, she was taking apart the crib he'd put together just a day before.

His heart beat erratically as he moved to his wife's side. "Kira, what's going on?"

Refusing to look at him, she continued her task. "We're not getting the baby."

His throat threatened to close up. No baby. "Why?"

She gave a shaky sigh and closed her eyes. "Darcy changed her mind." A tear rolled down Kira's cheek. "She wants to keep her baby."

It felt as if a huge weight landed on his chest, making it hard to breathe. No. He was just getting used to the idea of becoming a father.

"Oh, Kira." He reached for her but she avoided his touch.

"Don't." Kira climbed to her feet and moved away. "Don't tell me it's going to be okay because we both know it's not. It's never going to be okay, Trace. Not ever again." She swiped at the flood of tears.

Trace stood and went after her, but she continued to back away, his heart clutched in pain. Losing the baby was hard, but losing Kira was harder. Suddenly he felt his world being ripped apart.

"God, Kira, I know this hurts. We were warned this could happen." The words were so feeble. "We're still on the list. We can still have a baby."

"Another list!" she cried. "Then what? We wait some more and maybe have another baby jerked away again?"

Kira shook her head. She couldn't keep doing this to herself. Every time she began to hope, it was ripped away. And Trace. This had been their last chance.

"No, I'm not doing it anymore. I can't, Trace."

"Okay, we stop for now."

"No, I've stopped for good." Kira raised her gaze to his. There was pain in his beautiful gray eyes. It hurt her to know she couldn't be what he needed. It was time to stop it. "Your dream doesn't have to end, Trace. You can still have children."

He frowned. "What are you trying to say?"

She couldn't lose her nerve now. It was killing her to send him away, but better now than later when they ended up hating each other. She had to do what was best for Trace and the legacy he wanted to leave.

She straightened and wiped away her tears. "You can have the family you want, just not with me."

"I don't want a family unless it's with you."

She shook her head. "I can't keep doing this." She glanced away from his confused look. "And I can't keep putting you through this, either."

"You're not putting me through anything I don't want to do. I agreed to the adoption."

She straightened, fighting tears. "Well, I'm through." She stared at him. "Our original deal was for six months. We didn't get a baby, so you're off the hook."

"Off the hook?" He looked as if she'd struck him. "That's all you think of our marriage? That I came back because of the baby?"

She managed a nod, praying to stay strong. This was for the best.

Trace turned and walked out.

It was over.

With no desire to sleep, Trace took out his frustration by working through the night. By morning he had worked up a good anger as he continued his labor, mucking out stalls, repairing fence. He headed over to the foreman's cottage to see what needed to be done. Anything to keep him from thinking. Thinking about what he was about to lose. Everything.

He heard the sound of pounding in the foreman's cottage and wandered over to find Cal busy at work on repairs.

Trace maneuvered through the boxes stacked in the

small living room to find his foreman in the kitchen putting down new subflooring. He was surprised how much Cal had gotten done since yesterday.

"You're not wasting any time."

"Jody needs a place." Cal stood and pushed his hat back. "Since you've pulled an all-nighter, I take it things aren't good between you and Kira."

"We're not going to get the baby," Trace said.

He frowned. "So you left?"

"Sometimes we're not given a choice."

"And you're just going to give up?"

He hated to keep beating his head against the wall. "She's not fighting for me, either."

Cal sighed. "Marriage isn't a contest, Trace. It's hard work. Kira is hurting. She probably said things she didn't really mean."

"What are you, a marriage counselor?"

"No, but I've been there, dammit. I messed up big time. I walked away without fighting. It cost me my wife and my daughter."

"You have a daughter?" Trace asked.

"She's not mine anymore. I gave her up and I let my ex-wife's new husband adopt her. She'd be about Jody's age."

Trace watched Cal swallow hard.

"I regret it every day. Hell, Trace, I'd crawl back if I could have my family again, but I was too damn bull-headed to see anything beyond my pride."

Suddenly Cal glanced toward the doorway and saw Jody standing there in her jeans and T-shirt.

The teenager smiled shyly. "I'm sorry to bother you." She looked at Trace. "There was a phone call and

I heard the voice on the recorder. It sounded important, and Kira isn't around. Here's the man's name and number." She handed him a piece of paper, then looked back at Cal. "I hate to ask, but do you think you could take me to work?"

"Sure. What time?"

"In two hours."

He nodded. "Just come and get me when you're ready."

After Jody left, Trace looked at the note paper to see the name of Greg Carlson from the Teacher's Credit Union. Trace pulled out his phone and punched in the number.

It rang twice then was answered, "This is Greg Carlson."

"Hello, Mr. Carlson, this is Trace McKane. You left me a message."

"Yes, Mr. McKane. We wanted to let you and Mrs. McKane know that your loan has been approved. Since this is a joint loan, I need you to come in and sign some papers before we cut a check for Jarrett McKane."

Trace wasn't sure how to react. Kira had applied for a loan? To pay Jarrett? "Could you just put a hold on the paperwork until I talk to my wife?"

There was a pause. "That's not a problem. We can hold it for forty-eight hours."

"Thank you, Mr. Carlson." He flipped his phone closed. "Dammit, why did she do that?"

"Do what?" Cal asked.

"Kira got a loan to pay off Jarrett."

Cal raised an eyebrow and folded his arms over his chest. "Okay, now, tell me she doesn't care about the ranch. And you."

CHAPTER ELEVEN

THE next morning, Trace went to his brother's office downtown. There weren't any pleasantries or announcements as he bypassed the blond secretary and walked through the door. He found Jarrett on the phone.

The young woman ran after him. "Sir, you can't go in there."

His brother hung up the phone and stood. "It's okay, Sarah. I've been expecting him."

The blonde backed out and shut the door. "Well, it's about time you showed up," Jarrett said.

"I wanted the satisfaction of telling you, you're not taking my land. I was just with Frank Rhodes and signed a contract with EnRockies. You'll have your check for the land in plenty of time before the due date."

Jarrett shrugged. "You can't blame a guy for trying."

"Why, Jarrett? Do you hate me so much that you want to destroy me?"

"Hell, I don't hate you. I saw an opportunity and took it." Then his shoulders sagged as he leaned a hip on the desk. "The real estate market is a mess. I had to do something to save my business."

"If you'd let me know about EnRockies' offer from the first, maybe we could have worked together."

In his younger years, Trace had always looked up to his big brother. He was popular and a talented athlete in school. Trace had been shy and uncomfortable around girls. But Jarrett never had time for him. As adults, it had become a competition.

"Honestly, I didn't think you'd go for it."

"But you never asked. We're supposed to be family, Jarrett."

His brother didn't say anything as he studied him. "Did Kira talk you into signing on for this deal?"

The question hit a nerve. He'd never gotten the chance to talk to her. "She's with me on this. We're adamant about keeping the land. EnRockies' lease seems to be the best way to assure it. Now that section of land is mine free and clear."

Jarrett smiled. "You're married, bro, nothing is completely all yours, and since you're having a kid, you're going to need all the extra money you can get."

Sadness shook Trace. That dream was long gone. "There isn't going to be a baby."

His brother's smile faded. "Sorry to hear that. What happened?"

Trace found he was angry. "The biological mother is going to keep it." *And Kira doesn't have any need for me any longer,* he added silently.

"Okay. What's your next move?"

Trace didn't want to share his private business. "I don't have any." He suddenly felt defeated. "Kira's pretty upset."

"Which is understandable," Jarrett told him. "But there are other options out there."

It was strange talking to his brother about this. "Not when this baby was the main reason we've been together. Now that's gone."

Jarrett shook his head. "Nothing is gone until you let Kira leave. Come on, Trace, I know you're brighter than that." He smiled. "You managed to steal her away from me."

"Hell, I can't make her stay."

"Then give her a good reason not to leave," he began as he folded his arms over his chest. "Have you told her how much you love her, and that you can't live without her?"

Trace straightened. "What is this, Romance 101? I've tried."

"Seems to me a woman who goes out on a limb to get help so her husband can keep his ranch isn't a woman who doesn't care."

"Have you been talking to Kira?"

"No, but the credit union called about the balance on the loan. Like I said, a woman doesn't risk her future if she's leaving."

"That was before we lost the baby."

"So she just turns off her feelings for you?" He shook his head. "I don't think so."

Trace felt sad. "What about the baby? I can't fix that."

"No one expects you to, but hold on to her until you get another shot at it. You're going to have the financial means to pursue other avenues, too." He walked around the desk, sorted through his Rolodex and pulled out a business card. "When you're ready, give this fertility specialist a call."

Trace shook his head. "No, Jarrett. I can't handle this again."

Jarrett paused with a frown. "You can't handle it? What about Kira? Think what she's going through right now. And she doesn't have any family to turn to."

Trace started to speak, but knew it was true. Even he'd walked out on Kira. It had been her who'd come to him, begging him to move back to give her a chance at a baby. To give them a chance.

Even after he learned about the child she'd given up years ago, he felt hurt she hadn't shared it with him earlier. A revelation hit him. All along, he'd been the one who never gave her a reason to trust him. Maybe she felt she couldn't count on him to stand by her. And when she needed him the most, he'd run out on her. Again.

He glanced at his brother. "I need to get home."

Jarrett smiled. "Give Kira my love."

Trace headed for the door, praying it wasn't too late to do just that.

"You're not leaving town, or Trace," Michelle said.

That same morning, Kira paced her friend's apartment. "It's the only way. People won't understand why we broke up and I can't answer all the questions. It's the only chance for Trace to start over." She brushed a tear off her cheek. "He can find someone. Someone who can give him a family."

"What about you?" Michelle asked. "You deserve a life, too, Kira. A man who loves you. And don't try to say that man isn't Trace."

She recalled yesterday when she was so upset about losing the baby. He'd left her. "He walked out."

"Maybe because you didn't give him a chance."

Kira swung around to deny it and suddenly a wave of dizziness hit her. She reached for the back of the chair to steady herself.

Michelle rushed to her side. "You okay?"

Kira sank into the chair feeling a wave of nausea. "It's probably because I haven't eaten today."

"Great. Like you can stand to lose any more weight." Her friend walked into the small kitchen and took out some yogurt. "Eat."

Kira caught the aroma of the fruit flavor and her stomach roiled in rebellion. She barely made it across the room and into the bathroom before she lost what little food was in her.

With a groan, Kira leaned against the counter. Michelle handed her a cool washcloth. "Could this be more than lack of food?"

"Stomach flu. I haven't felt good for a few days."

Michelle gave her some mouthwash, then helped her to the sofa. "How many days?"

"Two or three, I guess."

"What are your other symptoms?"

"I haven't had any energy. Upset stomach, but a lot has been going on…with the baby and all."

Michelle's eyes widened. "And Trace has been staying in the guestroom since moving back?"

Kira felt herself blush. "Mostly."

"Okay, you better give me some more symptoms."

It suddenly dawned on Kira what she was asking.

"No, it's not that, could never be that. The doctor said it would be close to a miracle."

"I'm Catholic. We believe in miracles. My mother and I have had you on our novena list for the past year." She shrugged. "So why not? Are your breasts tender? When was your last period?"

Kira refused to answer, because she refused to hope. "It's too crazy to think about."

"It's not crazy."

She shook her head. She couldn't even hope.

"There's only one way to find out." Michelle grabbed her purse off the entry table. "I'm going to the drugstore." Before she could stop her, her friend was gone out the door.

Kira didn't want to take a pregnancy test. She'd taken dozens over the past few years and they'd all come back negative. She didn't need that today.

Ten minutes later there was a knock on the door. Thinking Michelle forgot her key, Kira got up and opened the door to find Trace.

"What are you doing here?"

Trace hadn't expected Kira to greet him with open arms, but he'd hoped for a warmer greeting. "I've been trying to find you." He walked in. "We need to talk."

"We've said everything, Trace. I'll be out of the house in a few days."

"I don't want you to move out. I want us to stay together."

She walked across the room. "For how long, Trace?" Tears flooded her eyes. "Until the next time I try to get involved in your life?"

"Can't we go back to the house and talk this out?"

She shook her head, fighting tears. "No, it's better this way. I'll come back another day when you're not around and move the rest of my things. And I don't want any part of the ranch. It was never mine."

"Yes, it is. The ranch is yours, too. You're my wife, Kira. I was wrong not to include you in all decisions concerning the operation."

He could only watch as she fought her emotions. "No, I don't want any part of the McKane Ranch. So just please go, Trace." She pointed toward the door and, as if by magic, it opened and Michelle walked in.

"I got you the last test at the drugstore." Kira's friend pulled a box from the bag. She froze when she glanced up to see they weren't alone. "Oh, Trace."

"Michelle." His gaze went to the box. He'd seen the same pregnancy test in their bathroom cabinet back when they'd been trying for a baby. He swallowed the sudden dryness in his throat as he glanced at Kira. Pregnant? Could she be pregnant?

"It's the stomach flu," she assured him unconvincingly.

"But you don't know for sure."

She didn't answer.

He went to her and took her by the arm. "We're going home." As they headed for the door, he grabbed the pregnancy test from Michelle.

"Good luck," she called to them.

Trace knew if he was going to have a chance to repair things between them, it was going to take a lot more than luck. He had to convince Kira that he wasn't going to give up on them. No matter what the test said.

CHAPTER TWELVE

THIRTY minutes later they arrived back at the ranch. Silently Trace led Kira through the house and upstairs to their bedroom, and into the connecting bath. Before she could argue, he set the test on the sink, then walked out, shutting the door behind him.

Kira relented and after the deed was done, she came out ready to give Trace a piece of her mind. "I don't appreciate you railroading me into doing this. The test will only show what we both already know." Her voice softened. "That I'm not pregnant...once again."

He got off the bed, but didn't apologize. "How long for the results?"

"Five minutes."

Kira released a breath and watched as he paced the room they'd shared over their five-year marriage. The memory of the night he'd learned her secret flashed into her head. The one night they'd made love and the times after that. Could they have made a baby? Could those nights in Trace's arms have created a miracle? She shook away the thought, refusing to let herself hope.

She straightened. "You go look, I can't go through the disappointment again."

He studied her. "It could be different this time."

"I don't want you to get your hopes up."

"Why not? After your last procedure six months ago, the doctor said removing the scar tissue could possibly help you conceive."

She sank against the dresser, trying to ignore the glimmer of hope. "Please, Trace, don't. I can't take seeing your disappointment again."

He walked to her. "Is that what you think? That I brought you back here just to find out if there is a baby?"

She was unable to look him in the eye.

"I brought you here because I wanted us to talk in private. So I could apologize to you."

"Why?"

"For walking out on you, especially yesterday." He paced as if agitated. "You needed me, Kira, and I felt helpless to do or say the right thing. When you pushed me away I was hurt. And maybe you won't believe this but I wanted the baby, too."

He sighed. "I wanted her for us. All I thought about was that little girl, how she was going to be the start to our family…the next generation." He forced a laugh. "I was looking forward to teaching her to ride, to rope and herd cows." When he glanced back at Kira, there were tears in his eyes, too. "How selfish is that?"

"Oh, Trace, that's not selfish. We all have dreams for our children."

He nodded. "Of course, she might have wanted to be a ballerina," he went on. "But none of that mattered, only that this baby would be ours."

"I'm sorry, Trace," she breathed. "At the beginning I pushed you into this adoption. Neither one of us was close to being ready for a family."

"That was my fault, too, Kira," he admitted. "I excluded you. You had a full-time job. I didn't think you wanted to be involved with the ranch, too."

She knew how hard it was for him to admit that. "I only wanted to share your life, Trace. Your love for the ranch."

"I wanted to share your past, too," he answered, his hurt surfacing. "No matter how bad it was for you. I wanted to share your pain." He went to her, gripping her arms. "I was never angry that you had a child. God, Kira, you were so young. What you did was so unselfish. You gave your son the best chance at life. No matter what it cost you. I guess my problem was I wished you could have shared it with me."

"I was wrong not to trust you. But I thought if you knew my secret, I would lose you."

He reached for her and cupped her face in his hands. "God, Kira. You could never lose me." He kissed her hard and long, and when he broke away, they were both breathless.

He moved back a fraction, but she could feel his breath on her face. "From the moment I laid eyes on you, I couldn't think of anything else. You had me spooked as a green colt. You have no idea how many times I drove to the school to see you, then stopped short of going inside. I'd turn around, drive back to the ranch and convince myself that someone as beautiful as you wouldn't want to go out with me."

His admission thrilled her. "It took you thirteen days to ask me out, Trace McKane. Thirteen long days."

He blinked at her statement, then he sobered and said, "I'm not good at saying all the fancy words, Kira. But you need to know that you're my life. You're all I ever wanted. The only woman I've ever loved."

With her heart racing, she couldn't speak.

"I was wrong to exclude you from ranch business," he went on. "My mother didn't get involved, so I took it for granted you weren't interested, either. And when things got tight, I didn't want you to worry."

"I wanted to help," she said. "I'm working, making a salary, too. Besides, you were spending ranch money on all my medical procedures."

"I'm your husband. It was important to me that I take care of my wife. But I admit, with the adoption costs and the balance due on the loan to Jarrett, it was going to be hard." He moved closer. "Then Mr. Carlson called from the credit union, saying your loan came through."

She shrugged. "I knew you'd be upset, but I only did it so you wouldn't lose everything."

Trace sighed. He'd never loved Kira as much as he did in that moment. He leaned down and brushed his mouth across hers again. "You're what's precious to me, Kira." Her brown eyes were luminous. "When I came back here this morning and found you gone, I thought you'd left for good. I've never been so scared. This ranch doesn't mean anything to me without you."

"But you can't let Jarrett take your land. Please, Trace, don't be too stubborn to take the money."

He smiled. "We don't need it now, as soon as you sign the papers, EnRockies will drill on the land."

Her brown eyes widened. "Really?"

He nodded. "It's time we had a little security for our future."

"Our future?"

"Yes, yours and mine." He slipped his arms around her. "Like I was saying earlier, I came looking for you because I wanted to convince you to give me another chance. Give us another chance. I promise never to walk out on you again." His gaze locked with hers. "We'll have rough times, but we'll work on them together. When you cry, I'll hold you. When you're hurt, I'll share your pain." He cupped her face in his hands. "We'll deal with the joys and disappointments together."

"Oh, Trace."

"I love you, Kira. Never forget that."

"I love you, too, but, children—"

"I told you before, Kira, kids would be a bonus. I married you to share my life." He sighed. "I guess I'm just going to have to prove it to you."

His mouth captured hers in a kiss he hoped would convince her just how he felt about her.

Kira was weakening, but Trace always had that power over her. His hands moved over her body; soon she ached with need. She needed him now as never before. She wrapped her arms around his neck and deepened the kiss. He groaned and yanked her top from her jeans and ran his hand over her stomach.

He broke off the kiss and whispered, "Tell me I haven't lost you, Kira. That you'll give us another chance."

"Oh, yes, Trace."

He lifted her in his arms as her mouth came down

on his. He carried her to the bed, set her down and finished undressing her as his mouth worked over hers, teasing her lips with his tongue. His fingers released the clasp on her bra and let her breasts spill out.

Kira arched her back as his hands cupped her, then his mouth captured the sensitive nipple. She gasped at the pleasure, but his tenderness caught her by surprise.

Trace raised his head. "Did I hurt you?"

She blinked. "Sorry, they're just a little sensitive."

He froze. "How sensitive?"

Kira knew what he was asking. She covered his hand and brought it back to her breasts. "Just a little."

"Damn. The test." He started to get up, but Kira wouldn't let go of him.

"Don't, Trace. Don't spoil this." Love and desire for this special man consumed her. "Stay and make love to me."

His brown hair was mussed, his beautiful gray eyes searched hers. He finally nodded and leaned down. "I promise you, Kira, someday we'll have a baby. It might take a little longer, but it'll happen. And together we'll raise our family. Here. At our home."

She suddenly felt pretty lucky. That's what she'd been looking for all her life. "That's all I need, Trace. Like you said, everything else is a bonus."

EPILOGUE

IT WAS late afternoon as Kira stood on the porch and watched volunteers set up the tables and portable barbecues for tomorrow's senior roundup. Although she'd taken off work the past year, she wasn't about to disappoint this year's class by canceling their party at the McKane Ranch. So tomorrow there would be about fifty kids and hopefully a lot of parents here.

Michelle had taken over the job of organizer, and she'd even roped Jarrett into helping out. The two seemed to be getting pretty close. So had the two brothers. Jarrett was even going on the roundup with Trace tomorrow.

She shifted little Nathan on her hip. The seven-month-old was getting big. She smiled at the cute little boy. It was hard to believe he'd grown so fast. He was thriving around his extended family.

"Here, I can take him for you."

She turned to see Cal coming up the steps. "I thought you were helping with setup for tomorrow."

Nathan reached out for his uncle Cal. "What can I say, I'm organized." He raised the boy high in his arms, causing him to giggle. "Besides, I promised Jody I'd bring Nathan to the house."

Kira was proud of Jody. She was working and going to college, plus raising her son. "She's supposed to be studying for finals."

"I know, but she wants to give him a bath and spend some time with him before he goes to bed."

Kira looked toward the foreman's cottage. The outside had been painted cream with burgundy shutters, and bright flowers lined the porch. Inside was nearly perfect, too. Cal had made sure of that. He'd taken both Jody and little Nathan under his care, playing uncle to the boy. It had been good for both of them.

"I'm worried that Jody isn't getting enough sleep."

"I'm getting plenty of sleep."

They turned as Jody joined them. She'd filled out since the birth of her son. The pretty girl was more sure of herself these days. Why shouldn't she be with all she'd accomplished this past year?

She was immediately drawn to her son. "How's my big boy?"

Nathan grinned showing off his two tiny teeth. She took him from Cal. After a series of kisses, she cuddled him close to her, and said, "I guess I needed a Nathan fix."

Kira's chest tightened. She understood the feeling. There was nothing like holding your child close.

"Then I guess…you can have a break," Kira said.

The girl started down the steps, then paused. "Have I told you lately how much I love you all, you, Cal and Trace? I wouldn't be able to bathe my baby every night if you all hadn't been there for me."

Okay, that made the tears fall as they thought back to the roundup a year ago. "And you're thanking us by paying it forward." After Jody graduated, she was going into social work to help troubled teens.

"I'm a long way off before I can do that."

Cal spoke up. "But the good thing is you're working toward it. And making us all proud."

Jody swallowed hard but didn't speak. Kira saw the emotions play across the girl's face. All her life Jody hadn't had many people behind her. Now she had a lot.

Kira waved to Nathan as mother and son left to go home. Their home for as long as they needed it.

Suddenly Kira's attention was drawn to the corral and to a lone rider. Her stomach got a funny feeling as she watched Trace sit atop Thunder. Her cowboy, husband and lover. Man of her dreams. All of the above.

When Trace spotted her, he tipped his hat and climbed down off the horse. He handed his reins to one of the two ranch hands they'd hired a few months ago. The extra money from the lease helped Trace expand the operation.

He started toward the house in his usual fitted Western shirt and faded jeans covered by rust-brown chaps. She knew he'd been checking the herd that was to be rounded up and branded tomorrow.

By the time Trace climbed the back steps, she felt breathless. Nothing had changed since they'd met. He still had that effect on her.

"Howdy, ma'am," he said.

She glanced over his dusty clothes. "Looks like you've been busy."

"I do have to work occasionally. I sure could use a shower." He stepped closer. "Care to join me?"

She smiled. "I might be talked into it."

His mouth closed over hers nearly before the words were out. The kiss grew deep and thorough, pulling her against him.

Suddenly there was a sound of a cry from the monitor on the railing.

He broke off her kiss with a groan. "Sounds like someone is hungry."

She nodded. "Okay, you go shower and I'll feed our daughter."

He started for the door, but paused. "Oh, I forgot to tell you that a John Kelsey and his son are coming by later to look at the bay mare, Sadie."

She paused. Trace had gotten into breeding horses this past year. He'd bought the bay mare with the idea of breeding her.

"This could be too good to turn down. Like you." He bent to kiss her again and the baby let out another hard cry.

"You better get her."

Kira raced up the steps and into the nursery. In the crib was four-month-old Jenna. "Hey, sweetheart, are you hungry?"

Her daughter whimpered as she waved her tiny arms and legs. Kira picked her up and cradled her precious baby in her arms. She was their miracle. After a quick diaper change, Kira sat in the rocker and unbuttoned her blouse. Once the child was rooted on her breast, Kira began to rock, looking down at the infant who resembled her daddy, but had her own brown eyes.

Kira closed her eyes, recalling the day she nearly lost it all until she let Trace talk her into giving their marriage another chance. They'd promised to love one another and to face whatever happened together.

The pregnancy test had been forgotten until much later when Trace came out of the bathroom holding the colored stick in his hand. That and wearing a big grin.

It showed positive. Kira had gotten pregnant.

After all the trying and praying and testing, she'd finally gotten pregnant. Little Jenna had been conceived the night Trace had learned about her past.

It hadn't been an easy time. She was high risk from the start, and the last few months had been spent in bed, but she carried their daughter thirty-seven weeks. Born three weeks early at a little over six pounds, the baby was thriving now.

Trace stood in the doorway, amazed at the sight. He blinked, hoping he wasn't dreaming as he watched his wife feeding their child. He'd never thought this day would come.

There was never a picture so beautiful, and so humbling. Kira had gone through a lot to get here, to have this baby. It took him a long time to understand. Then the day of Jenna's birth as the doctor put her in his arms, it all became clear. He never thought he could love so completely. Both his girls.

He walked in. "Mind if I join you?"

Kira smiled as she burped their daughter. "Sure." She switched breasts and soothed Jenna with a calming hand. She turned to him. "You look and smell a lot better."

He kissed her. "Glad you approve." He placed a kiss on his daughter's head, too. "I have plans once Jenna's had her fill."

Kira raised an eyebrow. "I thought you had someone coming by."

"We have time." He brushed a kiss across her lips, leaving them both wanting more. "I'll always have time for you and our daughter. You two will always come first."

"I know. A baby reestablishes your priorities."

"She makes me realize what's important in life."

Kira lifted the baby to her shoulder, patting her gently. It wasn't long before Jenna fell asleep and Kira carried her back to the crib.

Once the nursery door closed, Trace pulled his wife into his arms and kissed her. Their lips met as he removed her already open blouse. By the time they reached their room, she was half naked.

Kira couldn't have been happier or more turned on. "This is crazy in the middle of the day."

"We have to steal the time now wherever possible," he told her. "It's nearly five o'clock." He laid her on the bed and stared down at her. His eyes were filled with need and love.

"Have I told you lately how beautiful you are?"

"Yes, but feel free to elaborate." Kira helped him undress, her hands aggressively removing his clothes. His chest was broad and muscular, his waist narrow and hips taut and lean. His desire for her was evident.

Kira drew him down on her, loving the feel of him against her, also loving the precious words he whispered as he loved her slowly and completely. She clung to him, laughing and crying at the same time when the release came to them.

Trace pulled her to his side, not releasing his hold. "I love you," he said breathlessly.

"And I love you, too."

She sighed contently. "Our life is perfect."

"Just about," he said and kissed her forehead. He sat up on the bed. "But I'm hoping it's about to be."

Kira didn't know what her husband was talking about. He'd been showering her with gifts since they'd gotten back together.

"What did you do, Trace?"

"I guess you'll just have to wait about thirty minutes. Go take a shower and relax." He stood and began to pull on his jeans. "I'll listen for Jenna."

She didn't wait to be asked twice. She went into the bathroom, showered and shampooed her hair. After she dressed, Kira came downstairs to find Trace holding their daughter in his arms. He was talking to her, and she was making those cute sounds at him.

Trace saw her and his eyes brightened as he gave her the once-over. "Oh, darlin', you look good."

She glanced down at her black jeans and bright blouse, then glanced back at him. "You're not so bad yourself, cowboy."

He grinned. "Maybe we should go back upstairs."

"I thought you had a horse buyer coming soon."

He glanced out the kitchen window. "That would be John Kelsey." He took a breath and released it, then looked back at her. "That's not exactly the truth."

She stood next to him to see a car pull up in the driveway. "What's not exactly the truth?"

"John Kelsey and his son, Jack, aren't coming to look at a horse. They coming to see you, Kira."

Her eyes narrowed. Trace opened the door and guided her out to the porch. She caught sight of a tall man about forty-five. He smiled at her, then turned to the teenage boy.

Kira's breath caught when she saw the tall boy with curly blond hair and dark eyes. Her heart began to pound. It couldn't be. Not after all this time. She'd never hoped, never dreamed.

Tears flooded her eyes. She looked at Trace. "How? Why?"

Trace reached for her with his free hand. "You deserve this, Kira. It's time you met your son. Besides, Jack wanted to meet you, too."

She took a needed breath. "Really?" She couldn't move, but looked down at the boy waiting at the base of the porch.

Kira looked back at her husband. He had given her everything she'd been looking for all her life. He'd held out his hand to prove his support, his promise to share her pain and her joy.

"I'm here, Kira. I'll always be here."

It had taken a while, but she finally believe that he truly loved her. This was her home. "I know," she whispered, then took his hand and they walked down together.

As a family.

* * * * *

Celebrate 60 years of pure reading pleasure with Harlequin!

To commemorate the event, Harlequin Intrigue® is thrilled to invite you to the wedding of The Colby Agency's J. T. Baxley and his bride, Eve Mattson.

That is, of course, if J.T. can find the woman who left him at the altar. Considering he's a private investigator for one of the top agencies in the country—the best of the best—that shouldn't be a problem. The real setback is that his bride isn't who she appears to be…and her mysterious past has put them both in danger.

Enjoy an exclusive glimpse of Debra Webb's latest addition to
THE COLBY AGENCY:
ELITE RECONNAISSANCE DIVISION

THE BRIDE'S SECRETS

*Available August 2009
from Harlequin Intrigue®.*

The dark figures on the dock were still firing. The bullets cutting through the surface of the water without the warning boom of shots told Eve they were using silencers.

That was to her benefit. Silencers decreased the accuracy of every shot and lessened the range.

She grabbed for the rocks. Scrambled through the darkness. Bumped her knee on a boulder. Cursed.

Burrowing into the waist-deep grass, she kept low and crawled forward. Faster. Pushed harder. Needed as much distance as possible.

Shots pinged on the rocks.

J.T. scrambled alongside her.

He was breathing hard.

They had to stay close to the ground until they reached the next row of warehouses. Even though she was relatively certain they were out of range at this point, she wasn't taking any risks. And she wasn't slowing down.

J.T. had to keep up.

The splat of a bullet hitting the ground next to Eve

had her rolling left. Maybe they weren't completely out of range.

She bumped J.T. He grunted.

His injured arm. Dammit. She could apologize later.

Half a dozen more yards.

Almost in the clear.

As she reached the cover of the alley between the first two warehouses she tensed.

Silence.

No pings or splats.

She glanced back at the dock. Deserted.

Time to run.

Her car was parked another block down.

Pushing to her feet, she sprinted forward. The wet bag dragged at her shoulder. She ignored it.

By the time she reached the lot where her car was parked, she had dug the keys from her pocket and hit the fob. Six seconds later she was behind the wheel. She hit the ignition as J.T. collapsed into the passenger seat. Tires squealed as she spun out of the slot.

"What the hell did you do to me?"

From the corner of her eye she watched him shake his head in an attempt to clear it.

He would be pissed when she told him about the tranquilizer.

She'd needed him cooperative until she formulated a plan. A drug-induced state of unconsciousness had been the fastest and most efficient method to ensure his continued solidarity.

"I can't really talk right now." Eve weaved into the right lane as the street widened to four lanes. What she needed was traffic. It was Saturday night—shouldn't be that difficult to find as soon as they were out of the old warehouse district.

A glance in the rearview mirror warned that their unwanted company had caught up.

Sensing her tension, J.T. turned to peer over his left shoulder.

"I hope you have a plan B."

She shot him a look. "There's always plan G." Then she pulled the Glock out of her waistband.

Cutting the steering wheel left, she slid between two vehicles. Another veer to the right and she'd put several cars between hers and the enemy.

She was betting they wouldn't pull out the firepower in the open like this, but a girl could never be too sure when it came to an unknown enemy.

Deep blending was the way to go.

Two traffic lights ahead the marquis of a movie theater provided exactly the opportunity she was looking for.

The digital numbers on the dash indicated it was just past midnight. Perfect timing. The late movie would be purging its audience into the crowd of teenagers who liked hanging out in the parking lot.

She took a hard right onto the property that sported a twelve-screen theater, numerous fast-food hot spots and a chain superstore. Speeding across the lot, she selected a lane of parking slots. Pulling in as close to the theater entrance as possible, she shut off the engine and reached for her door.

"Let's go."

Thankfully he didn't argue.

Rounding the hood of her car, she shoved the Glock

into her bag, then wrapped her arm around J.T.'s and merged into the crowd.

With her free hand she finger-combed her long hair. It was soaked, as were her clothes. The kids she bumped into noticed, gave her death-ray glares.

They just didn't know.

As she and J.T. moved in closer to the building, she grabbed a baseball cap from an innocent bystander. The crowd made it easy. The kid who owned the cap had made it even easier by stuffing the cap bill-first into his waistband at the small of his back.

Pushing through the loitering crowd, she made her way to the side of the building next to the main entrance. She pushed J.T. against the wall and dropped her bag to the ground. Peeled off her tee and let it fall.

His gaze instantly zeroed in on her breasts, where the cami she wore had glued to her skin like an extra layer. A zing of desire shot through her veins.

Not the time.

With a flick of her wrist she twisted her hair up and clamped the cap atop the blonde mass.

"They're coming," J.T. muttered as he gazed at some point beyond her.

"Yeah, I know." She planted her palms against the wall on either side of him and leaned in. "Keep your eyes open. Let me know when they're inside."

Then she planted her lips on his.

* * * * *

Will J.T. and Eve be caught in the moment?
Or will Eve get the chance to reveal
all of her secrets?
Find out in
THE BRIDE'S SECRETS
by Debra Webb
Available August 2009
from Harlequin Intrigue®

We'll be spotlighting a different series every month throughout 2009 to celebrate our 60th anniversary.

LOOK FOR
HARLEQUIN INTRIGUE®
IN AUGUST!

To commemorate the event, Harlequin Intrigue® is thrilled to invite you to the wedding of the Colby Agency's J.T. Baxley and his bride, Eve Mattson.

Look for *Colby Agency: Elite Reconnaissance*

THE BRIDE'S SECRETS
BY DEBRA WEBB

Available August 2009

Harlequin® Historical
Historical Romantic Adventure!

REQUEST YOUR FREE BOOKS!
2 FREE NOVELS PLUS 2
FREE GIFTS!

HARLEQUIN®

Romance.

From the Heart, For the Heart

YES! Please send me 2 FREE Harlequin® Romance novels and my 2 FREE gifts (gifts are worth about $10). After receiving them, if I don't wish to receive any more books, I can return the shipping statement marked "cancel". If I don't cancel, I will receive 4 brand-new novels every month and be billed just $3.84 per book in the U.S. or $4.24 per book in Canada. That's a savings of at least 15% off the cover price! It's quite a bargain! Shipping and handling is just 50¢ per book.* I understand that accepting the 2 free books and gifts places me under no obligation to buy anything. I can always return a shipment and cancel at any time. Even if I never buy another book, the two free books and gifts are mine to keep forever.

114 HDN EYU3   314 HDN EYKG

Name   (PLEASE PRINT)

Address   Apt. #

City   State/Prov.   Zip/Postal Code

Signature (if under 18, a parent or guardian must sign)

Mail to the **Harlequin Reader Service:**
IN U.S.A.: P.O. Box 1867, Buffalo, NY 14240-1867
IN CANADA: P.O. Box 609, Fort Erie, Ontario L2A 5X3

Not valid to current subscribers of Harlequin Romance books.

**Are you a subscriber of Harlequin Romance books
and want to receive the larger-print edition?
Call 1-800-873-8635 today!**

* Terms and prices subject to change without notice. Prices do not include applicable taxes. Sales tax applicable in N.Y. Canadian residents will be charged applicable provincial taxes and GST. Offer not valid in Quebec. This offer is limited to one order per household. All orders subject to approval. Credit or debit balances in a customer's account(s) may be offset by any other outstanding balance owed by or to the customer. Please allow 4 to 6 weeks for delivery. Offer available while quantities last.

Your Privacy: Harlequin Books is committed to protecting your privacy. Our Privacy Policy is available online at www.eHarlequin.com or upon request from the Reader Service. From time to time we make our lists of customers available to reputable third parties who may have a product or service of interest to you. If you would prefer we not share your name and address, please check here. ☐

HR09R

You're invited to join our Tell Harlequin Reader Panel!

By joining our new reader panel you will:

- Receive Harlequin® books—they are FREE and yours to keep with no obligation to purchase anything!
- Participate in fun online surveys
- Exchange opinions and ideas with women just like you
- Have a say in our new book ideas and help us publish the best in women's fiction

In addition, you will have a chance to win great prizes and receive special gifts! See Web site for details. Some conditions apply. Space is limited.

To join, visit us at
www.TellHarlequin.com.

Coming Next Month

Available August 11, 2009

**Have a holiday romance with Harlequin in August
and get swept away by our gorgeous, sun-kissed heroes!**

#4111 CATTLE BARON: NANNY NEEDED Margaret Way
Scandalously gate-crashing her ex-fiancé's wedding costs Amber her
job! Then brooding rancher Cal MacFarlane makes her nanny to his
baby nephew. Once the media frenzy dies down, can Cal convince
Amber to stay?

#4112 HIRED: CINDERELLA CHEF Myrna Mackenzie
After an accident that shattered her spine, Darcy's made a new life for
herself as a chef. Her most recent position might be temporary, but her
gorgeous boss has other ideas....

#4113 GREEK BOSS, DREAM PROPOSAL Barbara McMahon
Escape Around the World
Aboard his luxury yacht, Nikos isn't looking for love. But sharing the
breathtaking beauty of the idyllic Greek islands with his pretty new
employee is driving him crazy!

#4114 MISS MAPLE AND THE PLAYBOY Cara Colter
Primary-school teacher Beth Maple is cautious and conventional. Yet
when stand-in dad Ben appears at the school gates with his good looks
and confident swagger, Beth is starstruck!

#4115 BOARDROOM BABY SURPRISE Jackie Braun
Baby on Board
When pregnant Morgan arrives at billionaire Bryan's office looking for
her baby's father, two things become apparent: she has mistaken him for
his late brother, and she's in labor—in the boardroom!

#4116 BACHELOR DAD ON HER DOORSTEP Michelle Douglas
Jaz is back in her hometown, determined to face her old flame Connor
with dignity—and distance. But she hadn't reckoned on Connor being
even more irresistibly handsome—or a bachelor dad!

HRCNMBPA0709